GOLDEN
GAME

GOLDEN GAME

David Starr

James Lorimer & Company Ltd., Publishers
Toronto

James Lorimer & Company Ltd., Publishers acknowledges the support of
the Ontario Arts Council (OAC), an agency of the Government of Ontario,
which in 2015-16 funded 1,676 individual artists and 1,125 organizations in
209 communities across Ontario for a total of $50.5 million. We acknowledge
the support of the Canada Council for the Arts, which last year invested $153
million to bring the arts to Canadians throughout the country. This project
has been made possible in part by the Government of Canada and with the
support of the Ontario Media Development Corporation.

Cover design: Shabnam Safari
Cover image: Shutterstock

Library and Archives Canada Cataloguing in Publication

Starr, David, author
        Golden game / David Starr.

Issued in print and electronic formats.
ISBN 978-1-4594-1231-6 (softcover).--ISBN 978-1-4594-1233-0 (EPUB)

        I. Title.

PS8637.T365G63 2017   jC813'.6   C2017-903303-4
                                                       C2017-903304-2

Published by: Distributed in Canada by: Distributed in the US by:
James Lorimer &   Formac Lorimer Books   Lerner Publisher Services
Company Ltd., Publishers   5502 Atlantic Street   1251 Washington Ave. N.
117 Peter Street, Suite 304 Halifax, NS, Canada   Minneapolis, MN, USA
Toronto, ON, Canada   B3H 1G4   55401
M5V 0M3   www.lernerbooks.com
www.lorimer.ca

Manufactured by Friesens Corporation in Altona, Manitoba,
Canada in July 2017.
Job #234938

To Constable Paul Starr, Corporal Andrew Starr and Corporal Jana Starr: the real Coach Ts.

Contents

1
The Accident

"When we're done shopping can I go to Dylan's house?" Abbas Wassef asked his mother.

"Help me get the groceries home. You can go then," Abbas's mother replied in Arabic. They walked down Grandview Boulevard, a busy street in their south Burnaby neighbourhood.

Abbas and his mother, Amira, weren't the only ones there who spoke Arabic, or any number of other languages. The sidewalks were full of people from a dozen different countries: Iraq, Ethiopia, Afghanistan and even other people from Syria, like the Wassefs.

Abbas loved shopping with his mother on Grandview Boulevard. It was much better than taking the Skytrain to the large grocery store at Metro Mall. He liked going into the *halal* butcher shop to buy chicken or lamb or to the greengrocer to get fresh fruit and vegetables. There was something about the small stores that reminded him of Syria.

Abbas knew every centimetre of the street,

every face, every odour. He knew they were almost home when his nose picked up yummy spicy smells from the Indian restaurant and his eyes saw the bright posters in the windows of the Filipino corner store.

Next door to the restaurant and corner store was the Persian bakery. Abbas's mom wanted to buy some *nan-e-barbari,* tasty Persian flatbread. It was to go with the shawarma they were having for dinner. Abbas's mouth watered. Mr. Mohammedi, the baker, made all sorts of amazing bread, cakes and treats. And he usually gave Abbas free samples.

Just before they reached the bakery, a terrible screeching sound filled the warm spring air. Abbas jumped as he heard glass breaking, the crumpling of metal and the shouts of startled people on the street.

A small red car and a large truck sat tangled together in the intersection of Salisbury and Grandview. They were surrounded by broken glass, and smoke was rising from the engine of the car.

Suddenly Abbas couldn't breathe. His heart thudded in his chest and his legs felt as if they were made of rubber. He fell to his knees, his head swimming. In a daze Abbas watched the driver, whose head was bleeding, climb out of the car.

Hall 2 of the Burnaby Fire Department was only half a block away. Abbas heard the sound of a siren as a fire truck pulled out. But Abbas wasn't looking at the fire truck or the accident, not anymore.

The Accident

Instead, he stared up into the air. His gaze went past the tall cherry trees with their pink blooms, past the roofs of the buildings.

"Where are the planes?" Abbas cried, his eyes searching the blue sky.

His mother knelt and held her son tightly. "It's okay, Abbas," she said soothingly. "There are no planes. It's just a car accident. We're safe. Everything will be all right."

2
The Invitation

"Great save!" called Dylan West, one of Abbas's soccer teammates.

"Thanks," Michael replied. He was the goalkeeper for their team, the Grandview Eagles, and he was on fire, stopping every shot that came his way.

It had been more than a month since the Eagles had defeated Regent Heights, Dylan's old school, to win the Burnaby School District Championship. But the boys still played soccer together every day at lunch. Today they played one of their favourite games. They pretended it was the final match of the World Cup. The game was tied and in penalty kicks.

"Now let's see you stop *me*, Michael!" laughed Claude.

Claude was a midfielder and Dylan was a striker like Abbas. Claude and Dylan were Abbas's best friends, not only on the team but in school as well. Claude placed the ball carefully on the penalty spot on Grandview's bumpy dirt field. "Top right-hand corner," he said, lining up his kick.

"Nice of you to tell me," said Michael, bouncing up and down on the goal line.

Claude grinned. "It doesn't matter. I have a feeling I will score. And when I do, Congo wins their first World Cup."

The other boys groaned. "You and your feelings!" said Mo. "You can't always be right."

"Just watch." Claude stepped up to the ball, raised his right foot and kicked the ball as hard as he could. The ball curved toward the top right-hand corner, like Claude said it would. It just missed the net, going above the crossbar by a couple of centimetres.

"I knew your feelings weren't always right," Mo said with a laugh.

Claude laughed right back. "Maybe, but that's the closest any of us have come to scoring on Michael today."

"Your turn, Abbas," said Jake, rolling Abbas the ball. "Let's see if Syria wins the World Cup this year."

Abbas took the ball. Today was Tuesday, four days since the accident on Grandview Boulevard, but he was still on edge. He'd not slept well since that day, and felt like he could snap for no reason.

"Are you feeling better?" Claude asked. Abbas nodded absently and forced a smile onto his face. All his friends had noticed he hadn't been himself. Abbas had told them he was sick. It wasn't a lie, exactly. But he couldn't even explain to himself why he felt so strange after seeing the car accident. So how could he explain it to his teammates?

Abbas kicked. It was an awful kick and he knew it as soon as his foot struck the ball. He watched as the ball spun harmlessly to the left, missing the goal by three metres. The funny thing was that Abbas didn't really care. All of a sudden soccer didn't mean so much to him.

"Wow, you must really be sick," said Junior. "That was the worst kick I've ever seen!"

Before Abbas could reply he heard a familiar voice calling the team. "Grandview Eagles!"

"Coach T!" The boys forgot all about the World Cup and ran toward their coach.

"How are you doing?" asked Dylan as the boys swarmed Coach T. They'd seen him just twice since the soccer season ended. Coach T was busy, because he wasn't just their coach. He was also a school Liaison Officer with the Burnaby RCMP.

"I'm fine, boys, how are you? Hey, Abbas! Second place in that big tournament for Syrian kids at BC Place. Not bad! What was the name of the team that beat you?"

Not long after Grandview won the school district championship, Vancouver hosted a large soccer tournament for Syrian refugee students. Abbas had been asked to play on the Herons, a team made up of Syrian refugees in Metro Vancouver. They came in second, losing in a shootout to a team from Toronto.

"The GTA Gazelles. Victor, an old friend from Syria, was on that team."

"The goalkeeper, right? I saw your interview. You looked great on TV!"

"What are you doing here, Coach T?" asked Jun, one of the team's best defenders. "Shouldn't you be at the high school, arresting teenagers for skipping class or something?"

Coach T laughed. He was clearly very excited for some reason. "You have all been given a very special invitation. And I'm here to deliver it personally!"

"Have you heard of a company called Electronic Arts?" Coach T asked.

"Have we heard of EA? Yeah, they make video games! *FIFA*, *NHL*, *Sims* . . ." said Michael, counting titles on his fingers. "They're like the most famous company in the universe!"

"Don't forget I'm old," said Coach T. "When I was your age we didn't have Xboxes, cell phones or even the internet."

"No internet? What did you do for fun? Play with dinosaurs?"

"Very funny, Claude. Dinosaurs were before my time. I played with woolly mammoths and sabre-tooth cats. Now are you guys going to make fun of an old man or do you want to know about the invitation?"

"Invitation!" they all said at once.

"Okay then," said Coach T, rubbing his hands together. "A couple of days ago I got a call from a man named Jon Lutz. He is the vice president of Electronic Arts in Canada. They have a game studio right here in Burnaby. Did you know that?"

The boys shook their heads as Coach T went on. "Jon read about the Grandview Eagles winning the school district championship and he was really impressed. He wants to meet you and give you a tour of the EA studio."

"Are you serious?" said Dylan. His jaw dropped.

"Us? Going to EA?" asked Carlos.

"One hundred percent serious," said Coach T, grinning. "Principal Bhullar has the permission slips in her office. If you want to go, that is."

"*If* we want to go? Are you crazy? Of course we want to go!" said Jun.

Even Abbas, who'd been feeling off since the accident, was excited. He didn't have an Xbox or a PlayStation but a couple of his friends did. FIFA was his favourite game of all time.

"Then get your permission slips from Ms. Bhullar, go home and get them signed by your parents. EA is sending a bus for you tomorrow after school."

3
Best. Trip. Ever.

The next twenty-four hours crawled by for the team. They thought they would explode with excitement when classes finally ended and a small yellow bus showed up at Grandview Community School.

"This is going to be so awesome!" crowed Dylan.

"How long will it take to get there?" Michael asked.

"It's a short drive," said Coach T. "We'll be at EA before you know it."

Within fifteen minutes the bus turned onto a street by the British Columbia Institute of Technology. It stopped at a gatehouse that had *Electronic Arts* written above it.

"The Grandview Eagles here to see Jon Lutz," said the driver.

"Welcome," the security guard said as he lifted the barrier. "Drive to the front door. Someone will meet you there."

"Pretty high security," said Abbas.

"No kidding," said Claude. "I guess they don't want anybody stealing the next edition of *Plants Vs. Zombies*!"

The bus stopped in front of a large building made of steel and glass. Two men and a woman stood waiting by the front doors.

"Welcome to EA," said one of the men. He was thin, wore glasses and was dressed in a casual shirt and jeans. He spoke with an English accent. "My name is Jon. I read about you in the newspaper and I wanted to congratulate you."

"My name is Wendell," the woman said. She was blonde and had a big smile on her face. "This is my assistant, Anthony." She introduced the young brown-haired man standing next to her. He carried a bunch of lanyards and nametags in his hands.

"Welcome, guys," Anthony said. "We have ID cards for each of you. Put the lanyards around your necks. You need to wear them while you're here."

"And one for you as well, Constable Whitebear," said Wendell once each player had his. "Now are you ready to have a tour?"

"Yes!" they all shouted.

Wendell grinned. "Then let's go!"

"We just finished renovating the place," Jon said as the team entered a large lobby. "What do you think?"

"It's so cool!" gasped Mo. All the other boys agreed. Ahead was another security barrier. To their right were two large doors.

"These rooms are new," said Jon, opening the first door. "We call them Right Brain and Left Brain.

Right Brain is a theatre and Left Brain is a conference room. Left Brain is pretty boring, but I think you'll like Right Brain."

Abbas couldn't believe his eyes. If Right Brain was a theatre, it was the best theatre he had ever seen. It wasn't that big, but it had about thirty large comfortable leather seats facing a huge screen at the front.

"We use this room to play games, to watch sports and show movies," said Jon. "When the European Championships were on, you couldn't get a seat in here."

"You let your employees watch soccer at work?" asked Claude in disbelief.

"Of course," said Jon. "We make video games about sports after all. You have to like video games and sports to work here."

"I do! Can I get a job here?" asked Alvin.

Jon laughed. "Learn how to code and we will talk."

"Okay, Eagles," said Wendell. "The tour starts now. Follow me."

"Coach Whitebear," Abbas heard Jon say before he left on the tour. "Would you mind chatting for a moment? There's something I want to speak to you about."

"Coach, you gotta see this place!" said Alvin when the boys got back from the tour. "We played *Madden* on a screen thirty metres tall!"

"They have a weight room and a sauna and a basketball court and a soccer field and so much cool stuff!" added Jun.

"We saw where they make games," said Dylan. "Wendell showed us how guys wear special suits so the computers can copy how they move."

"And we went to the cafeteria and ate donuts," added Claude. "Best. Day. Ever!"

"Claude ate about two dozen donuts himself," said Steven.

"You're one to talk," Claude laughed. "You had three dozen!"

Jon turned to Coach T. "Well? What do you think? Will you take me up on my offer?"

Coach T looked at the happy faces of his players. "Yes," he said. "I think it would really make their day."

"What are you talking about?" asked Junior, confused.

"Make our day? Nothing could make our day more!" said Mo.

"Actually something could," said Coach T. "Gather 'round, boys. Jon has something he'd like to talk to you about."

"I'm the chair of the board of directors of Canada Scores," said Jon when he had the boys' attention. "It's a charity. We focus on soccer, poetry and leadership skills."

"I know Canada Scores," said Abbas. "It's a soccer program at Grandview for the younger kids."

"Speaking of soccer," said Jon. "Have you heard of a tournament called the Top Flight Invitational?"

"No," said Dylan. "Why?"

"Top Flight is a big week-long tournament held at the end of May in Toronto. It is two tournaments, actually. The best U-14 soccer players are invited — sixteen girls teams and sixteen boys teams. Top Flight is run sort of like the NCAA basketball tournament in the USA."

"You lose once and you're out, right?" said Abdul. He was almost as big a fan of basketball as he was of soccer.

"That's right," Jon said. "Each team is guaranteed four games. But you have to win every game to advance to the final at Varsity Stadium, at the University of Toronto. If you don't win, you are relegated to exhibition games. Top Flight means the very best after all, and only the very best team will win."

"What has this tournament got to do with us?" Abbas asked.

"More than you think," said Jon. "A friend of mine runs a Canada Scores chapter in Toronto. He is also the organizer of the Top Flight Tournament. He's invited you to play in it. The board of directors of Canada Scores had a chat at our last meeting and we would like to pay for you to attend. We'll cover the hotel, airfare and food. What do you think? Do you want to go?"

4
Abbas's Problem

The boys were still grinning from ear to ear on the bus ride home. It certainly was the best day ever. One more chance to play together. And best of all, they would be playing in a superstar tournament in Toronto! Everyone was thrilled — except Abbas.

Abbas knew he couldn't go. The Top Flight tournament sounded great and the thought of seeing his friend Victor again was terrific. But the problem was in the very name of the tournament.

Flight.

Playing meant going to Toronto. Going to Toronto meant getting on a plane. And Abbas getting on a plane just wasn't going to happen.

All around him the rest of the boys chatted excitedly about the trip. Abbas said very little, lost in his own thoughts as the bus drove back to Grandview.

"Still sick, eh?" said Dylan. "How many donuts did you eat?"

"Too many." Abbas had only eaten one. The reason

he felt like he was going to throw up had nothing to do with food.

Ms. Bhullar was waiting as the bus pulled up. "Hi, Coach T," she said as the team stepped off the bus. "Anything interesting happen at Electronic Arts?"

Coach T grinned. "When did you learn about the Top Flight tournament?"

"About two weeks ago," she said. "Jon called me and asked what I thought about the boys going. I ran it past the school board and they were as excited as I was." She held out a stack of papers. "Today's Thursday. These permission slips need to be signed and handed back to me by Monday morning at the very latest."

"You heard Ms. Bhullar!" Claude took the papers and passed them out. "They might be due Monday but I have a feeling that we'll all bring them in tomorrow!"

Abbas took his permission slip. He stuffed it into his backpack and turned away, heading toward home.

"Hey, Abbas," Dylan asked, "You want to walk together? Give me a minute. I have to get something from class."

"It's okay," Abbas said. "I don't feel good. I just want to get home."

Leaving the team behind, Abbas walked across the gravel field. He headed onto Grandview Boulevard and toward the basement suite he shared with his mom in an old stucco house on Linden Street.

"How was the trip?" his mother asked. She was in the kitchen cooking dinner. The food smelled great. But with his stomach in knots there was no way Abbas could eat.

"Good," Abbas said, hoping mom his would believe it.

"You don't sound good," Amira said worriedly.

"I think I ate too many donuts," Abbas repeated the same story he told Dylan on the bus. "I'm going to lie down for a bit."

Abbas took off his shoes and walked to his small bedroom just off the living room. Shutting the door behind him, he dropped his backpack onto the floor. The thing felt like it weighed a ton even though it only held his soccer cleats, his school planner and the permission slip.

Abbas flopped onto his bed. The walls of his room were covered with posters of soccer players. They were all there: the Whitecaps, but also Cristiano Ronaldo and Gareth Bale from Real Madrid, Abbas's favourite team.

At Grandview there were kids from two dozen countries. But no matter where they came from they were either fans of Real Madrid or Barcelona. On the field they pretended they were Lionel Messi, Neymar, Gareth Bale or Cristiano Ronaldo, scoring the winning goal to win the league title, the EUFA Championship or the World Cup.

Abbas's Problem

It was Abbas's dream to become the first superstar from Syria to play in Europe. He wanted it not for himself but for his mom. She had had a very hard life. Abbas wanted to look after her, to buy her a nice house, to give her everything she'd never had.

Amira had lost a husband and two sons, Abbas's dad and brothers. They'd drowned trying to leave Turkey, to go to Europe to make a better life for their family. Abbas wanted to make it for them as well.

He slammed his fists down onto the mattress in frustration. The Top Flight Tournament was a golden opportunity. It could be the very thing he needed to take his play to the next level. Abbas should have been excited. Instead, he felt like throwing up.

If he couldn't get on a plane to fly to Toronto how on earth could he ever get on one to fly to Madrid, Barcelona, Paris or London? The answer was that he couldn't. His dreams would never come true. He would be a failure.

⚽ ⚽ ⚽

"I'm open! Pass the ball!" yelled Junior, streaking down Grandview's dirt field toward the goal.

"Here it comes!" said Abdul. He lifted the ball high into the air with a powerful kick.

The ball bounced once. Junior chested it down to his feet and in one swift motion drilled it above

Michael's outstretched hands. The ball zoomed into the back of the net.

"Abbas!" shouted Michael, booting the ball into the air. "It's coming to you!"

Just as the ball was about to land a siren started wailing. A fire truck pulled out onto Grandview Boulevard. Suddenly, for Abbas, the game, the field and the whole Grandview team seemed to disappear.

Abbas forgot all about soccer. All he could see was a collapsing building and a street full of burning cars. The cries and screams of people filled his ears. Abbas put his hands to his head, trying to block out the terrible sounds.

The images vanished almost as soon as they came. His head swimming, Abbas found himself back on the field. The sound of the siren was disappearing into the distance. The ball was bouncing on the ground in front of him.

"What's wrong, Abbas?" asked Alvin. "You just froze."

"Nothing! There's nothing wrong!" From out of nowhere Abbas's anger exploded. He shoved Alvin as hard as he could, pushing him down onto the dirt field. "Leave me alone!"

"Abbas! You stop that!" Ms. Shirley, the noon-hour supervisor, ran over. "Come with me to the office right now!"

In a daze, Abbas followed Ms. Shirley into the school, as the boys on the team watched in disbelief.

Ms. Shirley walked Abbas into the office. "You wait while I get Ms. Bhullar."

"Abbas! What's going on?" asked Ms. Bhullar, hurrying into the office. "Ms. Shirley said you pushed Alvin. Is that true?"

At first Abbas did not reply. He just sat there, his body feeling numb. "I . . . I guess so," he finally said.

Abbas had no idea why he'd pushed Alvin, or what had happened to him on the field. He couldn't have been seeing things, he couldn't have. The burning buildings and cars, the screams, they weren't real. Was he going crazy? Only crazy people see and hear things that weren't there.

"Getting into fights on the playground is an old habit I haven't seen in a very long time," Ms. Bhullar said. "I'm calling your mom. Something's going on with you and I think you may need some help."

5
Ms. Bhullar Knows What to Do

"Are you sure you don't want to go to the doctor's?" Abbas's mother had been in her English class a few blocks from the school. It took her just fifteen minutes to arrive at Grandview after getting the call from Ms. Bhullar.

"I'm fine," Abbas said as they walked out of the school. "I just have a headache."

"You haven't been feeling good for a while. Not for at least a week anyway. Please, son, tell me what's going on?"

What's going on?

Abbas hardly knew how to answer that question. He was going crazy, seeing things that weren't there. And then he'd hurt Alvin for no reason he could think of.

What's going on?

Abbas didn't understand it himself. How could he begin to explain things to his mom?

"I just want to go home and get some sleep," he said. "I must have the flu or something. My stomach hurts."

"Okay," his mother said reluctantly. "But if you aren't feeling better by tomorrow I'm taking you to the clinic."

As soon as they got home, Abbas went to his room and climbed into bed. His stomach did hurt, that wasn't a lie. It had been hurting for days now.

Abbas lay in silence for a while, falling asleep without knowing when he dozed off. It was almost eight o'clock when his mom opened the door and woke him up.

"I got a call from Ms. Bhullar when you were sleeping," said his mother.

"What did she want?" Abbas asked.

"She wanted to check up on you. And she asked me to remind you to bring the permission slip for the soccer tournament back to school on Monday. I told her I didn't know what she was talking about. Then I found this."

Abbas's heart sank when his mother held up a crumpled piece of paper.

"Why didn't you tell me?" she asked. "This is very exciting. You can see the Bayazid family, Victor and Gabriel and their parents!"

"I can't go," Abbas said. "It's the planes, Mom. I can't even look at one. How can I fly?"

"You were so young," his mother said sadly. "I thought you'd forgot about what happened."

"I've been having terrible dreams since that car accident on Grandview. I think I'm going crazy."

Amira hugged her son tightly. "You're not going crazy, Abbas."

"So what am I supposed to do?" Abbas had been carrying an awful weight in his heart. He felt better finally telling his mother. But still he felt helpless and scared.

"You are going to go to that tournament," his mother said firmly. "And you are going to see our old friends."

"I can't!" protested Abbas.

"You can and you will. You are going to go to that tournament. On Monday morning I will take the permission slip myself. Then we will sit down with Ms. Bhullar and tell her the truth. She will know what to do."

Abbas begged his mom not to sign the permission slip but Amira was having nothing to do with that. On Monday morning, as promised, she walked Abbas to Grandview Community School and greeted Ms. Bhullar on the playground.

"May we speak for a few minutes?" his mother asked. Before he knew it Abbas was sitting in Ms. Bhullar's office.

"We lived in Turkey for several years before my husband and sons died and Abbas and I came to Canada," Amira began.

The principal knew that much about the sad events that led Abbas to Grandview. "The war in Syria is terrible."

"More than you can imagine," said Amira. "The fighting was bad. But the worst thing was the bombing. That was why we left. I think that is also why my son has been acting strangely for the last week."

Abbas started to protest but Amira cut him off. "Abbas, she needs to know the truth so she can help you."

"Abbas was five when it happened," Amira continued. "I was in the market with him, buying food when the sirens rang out. It was a very busy street, full of people, market stalls and cars. Just people going about their business. Then the warplanes came."

"That must have been very scary," said Ms. Bhullar.

"It was. We knew what that sound meant, and we started to run. But before we could go very far the planes dropped their bombs around us. There was fire, smoke, screaming people." Amira's voice was shaking. "Abbas and I hid in a doorway and survived. But we saw terrible things that day. We knew we had to leave Syria. We got home and told my husband what happened. We left for Turkey the next week."

"You remember this, Abbas?" Ms. Bhullar asked.

"I don't like talking about it," Abbas murmured. He wished he was anywhere but Ms. Bhullar's office. "Can I go, please?"

"I didn't think he did," said his mother, ignoring

the question. "Abbas was very young. I thought he'd forgotten until we went to the airport in Istanbul to fly to Canada. He took one look at the plane and started to cry and scream. I could barely get him into his seat. It was not a good flight for the people around us, I'm afraid."

"Flying to Toronto has made you think about those planes you saw, hasn't it, Abbas?" asked Ms. Bhullar.

"I guess," Abbas said reluctantly.

"Then there was a car accident on Grandview last week," said Amira. "There was smoke and fire. When Abbas saw it he looked up into the sky for planes. I think it brought back the bad memories."

"I'm not crazy." Abbas was feeling defensive. "I'm not!"

"Of course you aren't," Ms. Bhullar said kindly. "How you feel makes perfect sense."

"It does?" Things didn't make sense to Abbas at all. How could they make sense to his principal?

"When people see something very scary or experience awful things it affects them. The word is *trauma*," Ms. Bhullar explained. "It can be a car accident or losing someone close to you or any number of things. I wouldn't be surprised if you are experiencing trauma right now. Tell me, Abbas. Since you saw the accident have you had bad dreams or scary memories that flashback to you at times? Have you felt angry for reasons you didn't know? Or nearly gotten into a fight with a friend on the playground, maybe?" she said with a knowing look.

Abbas was shocked. It was like Ms. Bhullar was reading his mind.

"Maybe," he finally said.

"There is a condition called PTSD. *Post-Traumatic Stress Disorder.* Have you heard of it?"

Abbas's face flushed. "No. And I told you I'm not crazy!"

"That's not what I'm saying at all," said Ms. Bhullar calmly. "You have some symptoms of PTSD. It is very common among people who have seen scary things."

"I don't have this disorder thing," Abbas argued. "I'm fine."

Amira reached into her purse and gave Ms. Bhullar the signed permission slip to attend the Top Flight tournament. "Here is the form, just like you asked."

Ms. Bhullar turned to Abbas. "You are going to be getting on that plane and you will be going to Toronto with the rest of the team. We have six weeks to get you ready and we will come up with a plan to get you there."

6
We're all Scared of Something

"Talk to the boys on the team," Ms. Bhullar told Abbas as he stood to leave her office. "They are your friends. They've been worried about you."

"And say what?" said Abbas. It was hard enough talking about this to his mom and principal. What would his friends think?

"Tell them you are afraid of flying," said Ms. Bhullar. "You don't need to get into the details. That's your business. It will be enough to explain why you've not been yourself. They will support you."

"I can't do that," Abbas said.

"I promise you it will go all right. Now go to class. Claude is the team captain, isn't he?"

"Yes, Ms. Bhullar," said Abbas.

"Ask him to schedule a team meeting this lunchtime. He is just the person to help you with this."

He didn't want to, but Abbas asked Claude to get the team together. They met, just the Grandview Eagles, in Ms. Jorgensen's room.

"Abbas has something he wants to say to us," explained Claude. "Are you ready, Abbas?"

Abbas wasn't, but it was too late to back out now. "I want to tell you all I'm sorry," he said, trying to find the right words. "I've been acting a little weird these days."

"You think?" said Alvin. He was the one who had been pushed by Abbas after all, and he was still upset.

"Let Abbas speak," said Claude. "This meeting is about solving problems, not getting mad at one other."

"I'm sorry, Alvin," Abbas said, and he meant it. "It's just that I'm afraid of flying. Since we found out about Top Flight I've been freaked out about getting on a plane. I didn't know how to deal with it. I took it out on you."

"That's why you've been like this?" asked Dylan. "We couldn't figure out what was going on."

"I didn't mean to be a jerk. But if you guys don't want to be friends with me anymore I would understand. Especially you, Alvin. I know I used to get angry and into fights a lot. I thought I'd changed, but maybe I haven't."

"Do you remember that first game against my old school Regent Heights?" asked Dylan.

"Of course," said Abbas. "We got beat 6–1. Our worst defeat ever. Your old friends weren't very nice."

"Forget the score and forget Tony and Emmanuel. Do you remember what you told me when I ran off the field?"

"Something like real friends don't treat you badly?" said Abbas, trying to remember.

"'True friends don't leave when things get tough. Friends support you.' I remember every word you said. That's when you told me about your dad and your brothers. That's when you told me that we were strong because we all found ways to overcome the things we have lost. We are your friends."

"You need friends right now more than ever," said Abdul. "We'll help you get through this. Besides, you're not the only one with fears. The thought of rats creeps me out. I hate them!"

"I'm scared of heights," said Alvin. "Flying is fine. But getting on a ladder or going up a tall building? No way!"

"Clowns," said Dylan. "The worst things ever. I watched this old movie on TV about an evil clown once. My mom said not to but I did anyway. I should have listened. I didn't sleep for weeks."

"Snakes for me," said Michael. "If I even see a picture of one I start to sweat. I imagine them jumping out of the picture and biting me."

As the boys on the team shared their fears with Abbas, he started to feel better, if only just a little bit. There was no way he was ready to tell the team why he was so scared of planes. But he felt as if he wasn't alone anymore.

"What about you, Claude?" asked Carlos. Everyone had shared their fears except their captain.

"It's nothing," said Claude, looking embarrassed.

"Come on, you can tell us," said Dylan.

"Okay. You promise not to laugh?"

"We promise," the boys all said together.

"Monkeys," Claude said, sheepishly.

"Monkeys? What about monkeys?" Junior asked.

"I'm scared of them."

"Who on earth is scared of monkeys?" asked Jun. "They are so cute and funny!"

"Oh no, they are not," said Claude. "They're dirty and scary and they make awful sounds. I got chased by one when I was a little kid in Congo. It bit me. I thought it was going to eat me."

"See, Abbas? We're all scared of something," said Dylan. "Now do we sit here all lunch talking, or do we get outside and play soccer? We have six weeks to go before the tournament and the only thing that scares me more than clowns is going all the way to Toronto and losing!"

When he got home Abbas went online and looked up the Top Flight Tournament. He hadn't known it was such a big deal. In it, thirty-two of the best soccer teams in the Greater Toronto Area competed until only one boys team and one girls team were left.

He looked at the list of teams and there were the

Grandview Eagles, the only team from B.C. The rest were from Markham, Brampton, Willowdale and other places he didn't know. There was, however, one familiar and unexpected name.

"Hey, Mom!" he shouted. "Come here!"

"What is it?" Amira asked.

"Hall United. That's Victor's school team," said Abbas. "We'll be playing in the same tournament!"

"Very exciting!" said Amira. "Perhaps you'll get to see him and meet up with his family. They were very close to us back in Syria."

"And maybe play him again too," Abbas said hopefully. "And this time win." The Vancouver Herons had lost in a shootout to the GTA Gazelles over March Break. Friendly tournament or not, Abbas didn't like losing.

Now there was Top Flight. This was a big deal, the most important soccer tournament he had ever had a chance to play in. He had to find a way to get on that plane.

7
Deportment Counts

"Now that's more like it!" shouted Mo as Abbas booted the ball into the net. The Grandview Eagles were practising after school. No one was working harder than Abbas. Since talking to his friends he had been able to play again. And more than that, he actually looked forward to it.

Ms. Bhullar said she had a plan to get him past his fear of planes. Abbas didn't quite believe her and he wasn't sure if he would be able to get on that plane to Toronto. But he could worry about that later. For now he would just play the game he loved.

"Great goal, Abbas," said Coach T from the side of the field. Abbas had told Coach T the same thing he'd told the boys on the team. He had a feeling Ms. Bhullar might have said more to Coach T, but if she had, Coach T didn't mention it.

"Let's practise some corner kicks," said Coach T. "Our set plays need some work. William, Jun, Steven and Alvin on defence, Claude and Mo can take the kicks and the rest of you go on offence."

The Grandview Eagles hurried into position, smiles on their faces. The boys really liked working on set plays. They knew that many of the goals scored in soccer come from corner kicks and free kicks. Besides, kicks were fun to do.

"Here it comes!" shouted Claude. Claude and Mo had the best kicking aim on the team, and in games they tended to take most of the kicks. With a solid *thump,* Claude's foot connected with the ball. It flew high in the air, curving gently toward the goal.

"Make the goal as small as possible. Stay out of Michael's way and get the ball away from the net," said Coach T.

Twin brothers William and Alvin took their positions by the goal posts. Their job was to get the ball to Jun or Steven so they could boot it out of danger.

"I got it!" shouted Abbas. He wasn't the best at heading the ball. But all the great players scored goals with their heads, and it was something Abbas worked on whenever he could.

As the ball neared, Abbas leaped into the air. His timing was off, and the ball glanced off the side of his head and out of play.

"Nice try!" said Coach T. "You almost had it."

Mo placed a ball on the arc but before he could take the kick, a police car pulled into the parking lot.

"Time out!" shouted Coach T. "Gather 'round boys,

there's somebody I want you to meet."

A police officer climbed out of the car. He was tall with short, grey hair and a long handlebar moustache. He was also wearing the fancy RCMP red dress uniform instead of the blue they usually wore.

"I'd like you to meet my boss, Staff Sergeant Major John Buis," said Coach T.

"Now *you* look like a real cop," said Steven, shaking the newcomer's hand. "No offence, Coach T, but we've only seen you wear your red uniform at Remembrance Day. And even then, yours is a little . . . boring compared to his."

"Look at all the stripes and stars and the pistols and rifle badges. How come you don't have any of those things, Coach?" asked Michael. "He looks like a general or something."

Coach T laughed. "Give me time, boys. Staff Sergeant Major Buis has been with the force for forty years."

"Your coach is right, lads," explained Coach T's boss. "I've been a Mountie for a very long time. I don't wear Red Serge every day, by the way. I'm on my way back from a citizenship ceremony. Welcoming new Canadians is important to me."

He unlocked the trunk of the car. "School sports are important to me as well. I'm more of a basketball person, but I really admire your team for what you've done. So do the rest of the members of the Burnaby detachment. We have a gift for each of you as you get ready for the Top Flight Tournament."

The trunk of the police car was full of shoeboxes and plastic bags. Through the clear plastic, the boys could see green and gold soccer uniforms and warmup suits with the Grandview Eagles logo printed proudly on all of them.

"You won't just be representing your school in Toronto," Staff Sergeant Major Buis said. "You will be representing Burnaby and indeed the whole province. You need to look professional. Deportment counts."

"Deportment? What does that mean?" asked Mo.

"Deportment is how you look and how you carry yourself. It's caring about your appearance and wearing your uniform proudly, whatever uniform that is."

"When we played Regent Park, Coach T told us it takes more than fancy clothes to be champions," said Carlos, one of the defenders on the team. "Do you remember?"

"Constable Whitebear was right when he told you that, young man." Buis handed Carlos a warmup suit. "Champions have courage, commitment and heart. But since you already possess those qualities you now need new gear. I'll not have a team coached by one of my members look shabby."

He handed out the gear to the excited players. "The fields you'll be playing on in Toronto are turf, and your regular cleats just won't cut it," he said as he passed out the shoeboxes.

"Thank you so much," said Claude, speaking on behalf of the team. "I can't tell you how grateful we are."

"The members of the detachment were happy to help out," said Buis. "Now get back onto the field and show me what you can do," he ordered.

8
A Surprise Appointment

"Where are we shopping first?" Abbas asked the next Saturday. He hoped it was the Persian bakery. He was hungry and Mr. Mohammedi made the most amazing walnut cookies.

"Later," said his mother. "Do you have your Compass Card?"

Abbas checked his wallet. "Yes. Why?"

"Because we're going to Metro Mall for an hour or so first." They reached the bus stop at the corner of Grandview and Humphries Street.

"What are we going to do at the mall?" Abbas asked.

"I need to get you some new socks. Half of them are full of holes."

"That seems a long way to go for a pair of socks," said Abbas. But before his mom could reply the bus squeaked to a stop in front of them.

"What else are we doing at Metro?" Abbas asked as the bus pulled into the Skytrain station five minutes later.

A Surprise Appointment

"My friend Maryam says there is a new restaurant across the street from the mall," Amira said. "It's supposed to be very good. A family from Damascus runs it. We'll go there for lunch if you like."

"Yes, please!" Dining out cost more than eating at home and wasn't something they did often.

"Train's coming. Hurry," said Amira.

They stepped off the bus and hurried to the entrance of the station, just a few steps away. Amira and Abbas tapped in with their cards and ran to the platform as the train arrived. They got on, the doors closed and the train pulled out of the station. Metro Mall was only two stations down the line from Grandview. They would be there soon enough, and the thought of going out for lunch made Abbas smile. He didn't much care about new socks, but lamb kebab and naan were something else.

But instead of entering the main doors of the mall, Amira led Abbas to a large office building next door.

"They sell socks here?" Abbas got a weird feeling as they entered the lobby of the building. "Mom, what's going on?" he asked as they reached the elevator.

"You have an appointment with somebody to help you with your fears," Amira said as the elevator door closed behind them.

"Mom!" Abbas was furious. His own mom had tricked him into going to some doctor. "I told you I'm not crazy! I don't want to go! This is so . . ."

"Enough!" Amira snapped in Arabic. She rarely raised her voice and the shock of it stopped Abbas mid-sentence.

"You need to talk to somebody about this," she said, more gently this time. "I'm worried about you and it is my job to get you the help you need."

The elevator stopped on the twenty-fifth floor. Amira led a sullen Abbas down the hallway to a door with a sign that said *Haval Ahmed Counselling Services*.

"Really?" groaned Abbas as Amira opened the door. "Do I have to?"

"Yes," she said firmly, "you do."

"You must be Abbas," said a tall, thin Middle-Eastern man. He was in his early thirties and had a scraggly beard. "My name is Haval. Welcome. Come in and have a seat."

Haval led Abbas and Amira into a small office. They sat on a comfy leather couch while Haval sat across from them in a large chair. "Now, what can I do for you?"

You can let me get out of here and go to SuperSports or Electro Video Games, thought Abbas.

"Abbas is supposed to go to a soccer tournament in Toronto, but he has difficulty with planes," Amira explained in Arabic. "His principal at school suggested we talk to you."

Ms. Bhullar! Abbas should have known she was involved with this somehow.

"So you're a soccer player, are you?" Haval asked,

switching to Arabic. "I'm a big fan myself. I used to play in university. I was pretty good when I was young, if I do say so myself."

Abbas looked at Haval. He doubted very much this guy knew anything about soccer. "Yeah? What is your favourite team?"

"Real Madrid. Who else? Thirty-two league championships, UEFA champions, Club World Cup Champions. They are the best."

Despite himself Abbas managed a small smile. "Who's your favourite player?"

"A lot of people choose Gareth Bale or Cristiano Ronaldo," said Haval. "They're pretty good. But I like Toni Kroos the most. Forwards get most of the glory but they need a midfielder like Kroos who can get them the ball. Kroos is hardworking and tough and nobody can pass better."

"That's true." Abbas and Dylan were the strikers on the Grandview team, but without Claude they wouldn't score at all.

"Your mom said you have to get to Toronto but you don't like flying. Is that right?"

"Did she say anything else?" *Like I'm seeing things? Did my mom tell you I'm going crazy?*

"We'll worry about that later. Let's focus on the plane thing. Your mom's booked five sessions. With a bit of luck and some work from you, I think you'll be able to get on that flight."

Golden Game

⚽ ⚽ ⚽

"Fears, such as fear of flying, are greater if your anxiety level is high," Haval explained. "From what your mom told me you have been feeling very anxious recently, so we are going to work on that. Does that sound okay?"

"Sure," Abbas said, not really meaning it.

"You're going to practise some breathing exercises and some guided meditation. It's easy. There is a great video on YouTube you can use. It only takes about twenty minutes a day and it really does work."

The homework Haval game him sounded okay in Haval's office. But when Abbas got home to his bedroom, he wasn't so sure.

He borrowed his mom's phone, went online and found the video. He almost didn't do it. Guided meditation meant listening to weird gentle music, the sound of waves and some guy with a soft voice telling him to breathe and relax. "*Clear your mind. Listen to the sound of the waves on the beach. Focus on your breathing. Feel your chest rise and fall,*" the voice said through Abbas's earbuds.

This is so stupid! What would the guys think?

Not that Abbas would ever tell the other boys on the team. He'd be so embarrassed he would never be able to show his face at school again.

A Surprise Appointment

But after about five minutes, Abbas started to relax. When the video ended he played it again. Halfway through the second time, Abbas fell asleep. That night he slept deeply, with no bad dreams for the first time in more than a week.

9
The Bulldogs Lend a Hand

"We're going to change up our practice location," said Coach T the next Monday. The team had been confused when they arrived at practice and were told to follow their coach away from the field. "I told you to bring those fancy new shoes to practice today for a reason. The ball bounces differently on turf and you're going to have to get used to that. I talked to the principal of Burnaby Creek Secondary. We're using their turf field today."

"That's great!" said Claude. Burnaby Creek was the high school most of the kids from Grandview went on to attend and it had one of the best soccer programs in the school district.

"There it is," said Junior as the tall lights that stood over the Burnaby Creek soccer field came into view.

"I thought you said we had practice," Carlos said. "There's a team already on the field."

"I have another surprise," said Coach T. "You've done a great job practising. But nothing beats games for training. So I organized a match between you and the Bulldogs, Burnaby Creek's grade eight boys team."

"Some of these guys are huge," said Alvin. He looked worried.

"It's not just turf you need to get used to," said Coach T. "You need to practise against older and bigger players to have a chance at Top Flight. Some of the guys you will play against in Toronto are already in high school. And high school starts with grade nine in Ontario."

"Are you sure this is the grade eight team?" asked Dylan. "They look bigger than that."

"They're grade eight," said Claude. He waved at a boy juggling a ball on his foot. "I recognize some of them. Hey, Martin!" He waved and a boy waved back and jogged over.

"Ready to get schooled, Claude?" Martin asked.

The rest of the Bulldogs came over to say hello. They all were glad to see Coach T, judging by the handshakes and high-fives.

The Burnaby Creek team was a lot like Grandview, seeming to have come from all over the world. But they were bigger — much bigger, especially a tall boy named Majok.

"He looks like a tree. A big tree," said Dylan.

"Majok's the goalkeeper," laughed Claude. "Not a lot of balls get past him. If you can score on him you can score on anyone."

"Okay, boys," said Coach T, "we didn't walk all the way to Burnaby Creek just to say hello. Put on your turf shoes and warm up. We have a game to play!"

The team pulled off their warmup gear, put on their new shoes and huddled around Coach T.

"I have a feeling we're not going to win this game," said Claude.

"Then it's a good thing we're not keeping score," said Coach T. "This isn't about winning or losing. It's about getting ready to play bigger, faster teams on turf. But I still want you to —"

"Play hard, play safe and play fair!" the boys chanted as one. "Let's go, Eagles!"

Grandview kicked off the game. Dylan passed the ball back to Claude as he and Abbas ran up the sides of the field toward the Bulldogs goal.

Claude was an excellent passer. If he got the ball forward to Dylan or Abbas, one of them usually scored.

"Abbas!" shouted Claude, kicking the ball high into the air. Abbas moved toward the ball to take it on the bounce. But once it hit the turf the ball bounced higher than Abbas was expecting.

Out of nowhere a tall, blond Bulldogs defender streaked in. He picked up the ball and in three strides was ten metres away. With a low, fast pass he sent the ball up to Martin, who ran like the wind, deking between Alvin and William. The Grandview players looked like they were standing still.

The Bulldogs Lend a Hand

From near the penalty spot, Martin took a sharp kick. The ball sliced through the air and slammed into the back of the net.

"Nice try, Michael," Coach T called to the Eagles goalkeeper. "Nothing you could have done! Now let's get that one back, Eagles!"

"Lesson one," said Shane, the defender who'd taken the ball from Abbas. "The ball bounces higher on turf. Give yourself more space."

The Eagles started playing more carefully. Instead of booting the ball up to strikers Dylan or Abbas, midfielder Claude made a short pass to Mo, who kicked the ball up to Dylan.

Dylan was fast. There were two Bulldogs defenders between him and the net. Dylan saw the gap between them and rushed toward the empty space.

Abbas had seen Dylan split defenders more times than he could remember. He ran to get in front of the net. Dylan would get past these defenders and lob the ball toward Abbas. Abbas would beat the last man back and score.

But the two Bulldogs defenders seemed to have read Dylan's mind. A wiry Iranian boy Claude had called Omid cut off Dylan, and with a beautiful slide tackle stripped him of the ball. Omid scrambled back to his feet and passed the ball down the field toward the Bulldogs midfielders.

"Nice try," Omid said as play continued, "but your

eyes showed me exactly what you were planning to do. Don't give away your play."

Twenty minutes and several Bulldogs goals later, Coach T blew the whistle at the half. The Grandview Eagles walked off the field and threw themselves down on the sideline. They slurped thirstily from their water bottles.

"I feel like I just ran a marathon," wheezed Carlos.

"Have a drink and a quick rest," said Coach T. "Because if this is a marathon it's only half over!"

The second half started just like the first. The Bulldogs were bigger, stronger and faster than the Eagles. Soon they had scored two more goals. The first was an amazing strike by a big midfielder named Garrett.

The other goal was less impressive. Martin crossed in the ball from near the sidelines. It bounced on the ground in front of Michael, who jumped up to catch it. But, still getting used to the new shoes and the turf, Michael slipped and missed. The ball rolled past him into the net.

Abbas groaned. He hated to lose, even a scrimmage against the high school kids. Coach T said no one was keeping score but it bugged him that the Eagles couldn't even get one lousy goal.

Junior kicked off, sending it back to Alvin. As the

Bulldogs strikers ran at him he passed the ball back to Alvin, who sent it smartly up to Claude.

"Coming to you, Dylan," Claude said. Dylan was tired, but he sprinted past a surprised Bulldogs midfielder, and was soon open on the left wing.

The ball flew through the air, landing just in front of Dylan. It was a perfect pass from Claude. Dylan guessed where the ball would land, picked it up on his left foot and hurried downfield.

Three Bulldogs defenders chased him into the corner. One of them moved in to tackle Dylan. Dylan tried to deke around him, and almost got clear. But just as he was about to send the ball to Abbas, a Bulldog foot came out of nowhere and knocked the ball out of bounds.

Tweet! The referee pointed to the corner. Dylan had earned the Eagles their first corner kick of the game.

"This is our chance," said Claude. Abbas, Dylan, Junior and Steven lined up across the mouth of the goal waiting for the kick. The whistle blew and the ball shot into the air.

"I got it!" Dylan shouted. But the ball sailed high over his head.

Abbas jumped and turned his head toward the approaching ball. He closed his eyes, waiting for the ball to hit his forehead. Instead, it glanced off the top of his head and flew high into the air toward the Bulldogs net. Majok easily reached up and punched it over the net and out of touch.

"Watch your timing," Majok said to Abbas. "You jumped too late. You need to get your forehead on the ball. Then you push it with your head toward the target. And keep your eyes open. You can't hit what you can't see."

"Let's try that again," said Claude as he placed the ball for the second corner kick. This one went higher and faster than the first one, and came right to Abbas.

Watch your timing.

With the ball just a few metres away, Abbas jumped into the air. He fought the urge to close his eyes until after he thumped the ball cleanly with his forehead.

Abbas sent the ball low, toward the right corner of the net. Majok threw himself toward it, punching the ball out of bounds. "Much better!" said Majok, climbing to his feet. "You had me beat."

"But I missed the goal," said Abbas, shaking his head.

"You just got unlucky," Majok said. Your jump was great and your timing even better. That was a good try. Maybe you can play with the big kids after all!"

10

More in Common Than You Know

"So how is the soccer going?" Haval asked in Arabic. It was their third session, and at the end of their second session Abbas had told Haval how the team was getting ready for the tournament.

"Really well," Abbas replied. "We've played against the grade eight team twice. The first time they beat us pretty bad. We didn't even score. This week we only lost by three goals."

It *was* going well. Abbas loved soccer, he truly did. And playing with his friends made him want to work on his fear of flying more than anything. He needed to be able to play in the Top Flight Tournament with them.

"Good," said Haval. "You'll be ready for this tournament in no time. And the meditation?"

"At first I thought it was kind of stupid. But it actually works," Abbas admitted.

Haval smiled. "How many times a week are you doing it?"

"Four, maybe five. Not every day. I have soccer practice too. Is that okay?"

"More than okay. Getting over fears is a lot like soccer. There is no magic cure, just lots of practice. You practise your set plays like corner kicks just like you practise your relaxation. If you work on both you will be more than ready to not only get on that plane but do really well in the tournament too. And speaking of practice, we are going to do some muscle-relaxing exercises today."

Haval had Abbas take off his shoes. "When people are stressed it isn't just their minds that feel it," Haval explained. "Their bodies react and often they don't even know it. Their muscles get all tense. They are sore and don't sleep well. They can even get stomach aches. Does that sound familiar?"

"I guess." It was kind of freaky when Haval seemed to know exactly how Abbas was feeling.

"Take a few deep breaths," said Haval, "then flex your left foot downward. Stretch the toes as far as you can. Hold them for about five seconds and then relax the muscles, breathing out as you do."

"What's that supposed to do?"

"Just trust me," said Haval. "Now lift your toes up until you feel the squeeze in your calf."

Abbas focused on doing what Haval was telling him to do, even though it sounded kind of silly.

"Now squeeze and relax each muscle group in your left leg," Haval continued. "And then do the same on your right. After that you keep moving up your body until you reach the top of your head. Ready to try?"

With Haval leading him, Abbas squeezed then relaxed all the muscles in his body. He worked the muscles one after the other, right up to his forehead.

"How do you feel?" Haval asked when Abbas was done.

"Tired, sore and relaxed all at once," Abbas said.

"That's exactly how you should feel. As well as the meditation I want you to do this exercise at least twice a day. The great thing about it is that you can do it at school in your desk and nobody will even know."

"Where did you learn how to do all this stuff?" Abbas asked.

"At the University of British Columbia. I was going to be a chemistry teacher. My parents were both science professors back in Iraq. I wanted to teach as well, to work with kids. But then I took a psychology class and realized that maybe I could do more for kids than teach chemistry."

"You lived in Iraq?" Abbas knew Haval's family had come from somewhere in the Middle East. But Haval spoke perfect English, and Abbas thought he had been born in Canada.

"I was ten when we moved to Canada. I'm a Kurd and Baghdad was pretty dangerous for Kurds. My parents wanted me and my sister to be safe so they turned to the United Nations for help."

"You were a refugee too?" Abbas was surprised.

"We have more in common than you know. I came to Canada not speaking any English. My parents couldn't teach here. So my dad got a job at a grocery store and my mom cleaned houses."

"My mom was a scientist and my dad was an engineer in Syria," Abbas said. "My mom is going to school for English. My dad and brothers died before we got here."

Haval nodded. "When I first got to Canada I was pretty messed up. I saw all sorts of bad things back home. Fighting, car bombings, you name it." He looked at Abbas. "Just like you, right? Your fear of planes isn't only about flying on them, is it?"

Abbas struggled to control his emotions. "Did my mom tell you that?"

"A little bit, yes. Do you want to talk about it?"

To his surprise, Abbas did. He sat in the comfy leather chair in Haval's office and told him everything. He talked about his memories of the bombing attack in the market, the trip to Turkey and the death of his father and brothers.

Abbas spoke about his trouble adjusting to life in Canada, getting to know his friends and the soccer team. Finally, Abbas told Haval about the car crash that seemed to have brought the bad memories back.

Haval listened, not saying a single word.

"That is quite the story," Haval said when Abbas

was done. "You did a good job telling it. How do you feel now?"

Speaking about those things was very hard for Abbas. "I feel tired," Abbas said.

"I'm not surprised," Haval said. "This is hard work. We've got two more sessions left. After them, I know you'll be able to get on that plane with your friends. But before you go today I have a gift for you."

Haval stood up and got a bag out of the drawer in his desk. "An iPod and noise-reducing headphones," he said, handing the bag to an awestruck Abbas. "Your mom said you were using her phone to do the meditation. I want you to do it every day from now on, and even when you are away. You'll need your own stuff."

"Thank you," said Abbas, gratefully.

"It's not the newest player but it works fine. I've downloaded a bunch of guided meditations and some music for relaxing and a bunch of apps and games as well."

"Is there a waves crashing on the beach app?"

Haval laughed. "Along with singing whale apps, chirping bird apps and falling rain apps. All very soothing. You should share them with your friends."

"No thanks," said Abbas, grinning. "If the guys heard me singing along to whale music I'd have bigger problems than a fear of planes!"

11
Ready to Play

The last week of May was wet and grey. Rain fell almost every day but it did not dampen the excitement the Grandview Eagles felt. The team was almost ready.

They'd played nearly every day since learning about Top Flight. The plane tickets were booked for Thursday morning. All that was left was the Tuesday practice game against the Burnaby Creek Bulldogs.

"This time we're keeping score," said Coach T as the Eagles reached Burnaby Creek Secondary.

"I thought you didn't care about beating these guys," Claude said, smiling. "Keeping score means you care."

"I don't. This is about practising your skills."

"Really?"

"Okay," Coach T admitted with a grin. "Maybe I care. A little. Get out there and show me what you can do."

"Go Eagles!" shouted Mo as the rest of the team joined in. "Play hard! Play safe! Play fair!"

The Eagles were playing the best soccer they had ever played. The Bulldogs scored on a wicked shot by

Martin. But the Eagles were hanging on. The score was 1–0, and would have been tied if not for an amazing save by Majok on a breakaway by Claude.

The half-time whistle blew. The Eagles hurried off the field, tired but confident. *The Bulldogs are worried*, Abbas thought. He could tell by looking at them. They weren't joking and smiling when they went to the sidelines.

"You're doing great," said Coach T.

"Thanks," said Abbas. He thought so too. The first time the Eagles played the Bulldogs they had been crushed. Now they were holding their own.

The second half was a chess match. Ball possession was split almost evenly between the two teams. Both had chances but nobody scored. With only a few minutes left the Bulldogs focussed on defence. There was no way they were going to lose to an elementary school team.

On the Bulldogs side of centre, Junior and Claude surrounded Bulldogs midfielder Garrett. Garrett tried to dribble out of danger and pass the ball, but Claude stretched out his toe, breaking up the pass. Claude deflected the ball to Junior, who turned and ran.

Five paces later Junior lifted the ball high into the air toward Dylan, over the heads of the Bulldog defenders.

Dylan ran up to the ball. He judged the bounce perfectly and quickly controlled the ball with his feet. One defender and Majok were the only Bulldogs between him and tying the game.

Abbas sprinted into the middle of the field, making sure to stay onside.

Dylan saw him, faked to the left then kicked the ball across the field. It was a fast, low kick that flew over the turf like a puck on ice.

Abbas streaked toward Majok. The Bulldogs goalie came out to meet him, cutting off the angle. His long arms were spread out, his feet bouncing up and down.

With a mighty kick Abbas sent the ball high, toward the left-hand side. Majok saw what was happening and stretched out his long body, but the ball was too fast. Majok fell to the ground as the ball crossed the line.

The Grandview Eagles swarmed Abbas, hugging him and lifting him up into the air. Coach Faraguna, the Bulldogs coach, was refereeing. He looked at his watch and blew the whistle.

Game over. The score was 1–1. But as far as the Eagles were concerned it wasn't a tie. It was one of the greatest wins they'd ever had, as good, maybe even better than the one that got them the District Championship.

The two teams lined up and shook hands.

"I didn't see that one coming," said Majok to Abbas. "Good luck in Toronto."

A jubilant Eagles team gathered up their things and started to walk back to Grandview Community School.

"No practice tomorrow," said Coach T. "You need to rest and pack your things. I want you all to wear your warmup gear on the plane. You are representing your school and your city. Deportment counts, remember?"

"Don't worry, Coach T," said Claude. "We're gonna be the best-looking team at the tournament."

"What time is the flight?" Mo asked.

"The plane leaves at 10:15 a.m. Make sure you are at the school for 7:30 at the latest. We need to be at the airport two hours before we take off."

"You heard Coach T," said Claude. "Not one minute later than 7:15."

"Make sure you pack your shoes and your uniforms as well," Coach T said. "And plenty of spare socks and underwear. Looking good doesn't mean much if you smell!"

The night before the Eagles flew to Toronto, Dylan and his mom, Erin, had Abbas, Amira, Claude and his sister Julie to their home for dinner.

"I said I was cooking spaghetti! You didn't need to bring anything," said Erin as their guests arrived at the Wests' small apartment on Salisbury Street.

"I know," said Amira, handing Erin a warm bowl. "But the boys love chicken shawarma so I just had to make some."

"And fried plantains too!" said Julie. She did the cooking for Claude and herself, and knew the boys shared a love of food.

"We have enough food for the entire team here!" said Erin, welcoming her company inside.

"Don't worry, Mrs. West," said Claude. "I have a feeling there won't be many leftovers!"

"How's school going?" Erin asked Julie. Claude's older sister was studying to be a nurse.

"I will be done in September," she said. "I can't believe how fast it went. I'll have to start looking for a job so I can pay off my student loans."

"Don't worry about that," Erin replied. "Nurses are in demand. You should find a job no problem."

The food was great and the company terrific but Abbas didn't feel like eating nearly as much as his friends.

Abbas had been practising his meditation and muscle-relaxing exercises. But he was still very nervous. In less than twenty-four hours he was supposed to be climbing onto a plane. Even with everything he'd done to prepare, Abbas wasn't certain he could do it. But the only thing worse than flying would be letting his friends and team-mates down.

"Come on, Abbas, have more of my mom's meatballs," said Dylan. "They are the best in the entire world!"

"How are you feeling about the flight tomorrow, Abbas?" Claude asked.

"Nervous. I haven't told you guys this yet. I've been seeing somebody to learn strategies to help me get over my fears."

Amira patted her son's hand proudly. She hadn't told anyone Abbas was getting counselling. She knew that telling his friends showed how far he had come. Perhaps one day he would be able to tell them where the fear really came from.

"Good thing," said Dylan, "because if you don't get on that plane you won't get to see your friend Victor. And we won't have a chance of winning Top Flight."

"And you should eat more," Claude added. "We're going to fly across the country, play four games and fly home. All in less than a week. You're going to need your energy!"

12
Ready to Fly

Abbas felt he hardly slept a wink all night. And that was after doing his muscle-relaxing exercises and listening half a dozen times to the guided meditations. But he must have fallen asleep somehow, because before Abbas knew it his mom had come into his room to wake him.

"Ready to go?" Amira asked.

"I don't really know." Not going meant turning his back on his team, his old friend Victor and the game he loved. Abbas would do his best not to let that happen.

"You can do this, son," Amira said. "I'm very proud of you. Now come and eat some breakfast. It's seven. We need to leave in fifteen minutes."

Abbas tried to eat but all his stomach could manage was half a bowl of cereal.

"Let's get going, then," Amira said. She brought Abbas's small suitcase to the door. "I'll walk with you to school this morning."

"You don't have to," protested Abbas.

"I won't see you for a week," Amira said. "That's the

longest I've been away from you in my life. If I want to walk you to the school I will."

Amira gave Abbas a small plastic card. "This is your Permanent Resident Card, your identification for the flight. For goodness sake don't lose it."

Abbas looked at the picture. It was taken three years before when he had first arrived in Canada. A great deal had happened since then. "Don't worry. Coach T said he'd look after all our ID. Apparently he doesn't trust us any more than you do."

By 7:30 all the Grandview Eagles players were at the school. Ms. Bhullar was waiting for them, along with Coach T, the bus and two other familiar faces.

"Good luck, boys," said Jon Lutz from Electronic Arts. "I wanted to see you off."

"You look very sharp in those track suits," said Staff Sergeant Major Buis. "Deportment counts after all."

"Okay, Eagles," said Coach T. "I want to make sure each of you has your ID as well as your uniforms. You're going to need both to play in this tournament."

The team handed their IDs to Coach T, who put them safely into his briefcase. Most of the boys had Permanent Resident Cards, but some had Citizenship Cards or passports.

"Uniform check next," Coach T said. "Show me you each have your jerseys, shorts and socks."

One by one the boys showed Coach T their green and yellow Grandview Eagles jerseys.

Just before they boarded the bus, Amira gave Abbas the biggest hug he'd ever had. "You have Victor's contact information?" she asked.

"Yes, Mom. I'll talk to him when I get there."

"I love you, son," Amira said, letting Abbas go. "You can do this."

"I hope so," Abbas said, "because if I can't you're going to get a call from the airport to come and pick me up."

⚽ ⚽ ⚽

"We'll be there in thirty minutes," said Coach T as he took a seat beside Abbas. "How are you doing?"

"I'm trying not to think about it."

"Then let's talk about soccer. Did you see the Whitecaps game last week?"

Soccer was a good topic. That was, after all, why Abbas was going to Toronto. They were still talking about the game when the bus got close to the airport. The sound of a large jet engine came from overhead. Abbas winced. Sweat formed on his head.

Breathe, breathe, you can do this, Abbas said to himself, fighting his nerves.

"We'll be at the gate in one minute," the bus driver. "Good luck in Toronto."

The bus stopped outside the domestic terminal. The Eagles followed their Coach inside to the counter where they were met by an airline agent.

"Grandview Eagles," said a young woman with a big smile. "We've been expecting you."

"You have their tickets and IDs, Coach?"

"Of course," Coach T replied. He took the cards and passports out of his briefcase, along with a stack of printed tickets.

One by one the boys took their IDs and tickets from Coach T and showed them to the WestJet agent. "Good luck, boys," she said and smiled again when the last of them had been checked in. "I hope you do really well. Have you flown to Toronto before?"

"I've never flown anywhere before!" said Michael.

Michael was the only one. All the other boys had been on a plane before. But most of them hadn't flown since arriving in Canada and only a handful could remember the trip.

"Well then I hope your first flight is one you will never forget."

I hope this flight is one I forget about quickly, Abbas thought. He patted his jacket pocket, making sure the iPod was there. He would need all of the meditations to make it through, he was certain of it.

The boys joined the line of people snaking its way toward the security check.

"You've got this, Abbas," said Claude. "Are you working on those strategies you talked about the other night?"

Abbas clenched then unclenched his fist. "I'm trying to," he said, "believe me."

It was Abbas's turn to go through security. He took off his jacket, put his backpack on the conveyor belt and walked through the metal detector.

"This airport is like a museum!" said Mo, looking around. Vancouver International was a beautiful airport, full of First Nations totem poles, carvings and murals.

"Here we are, boys," said Coach T as they got to the waiting area. "Gate Forty-three. There's our plane."

It took Abbas everything he had to look out the window. There it was, the long white plane with blue and green lettering on its side.

Breathe. You can do this, Abbas said to himself again.

The plane didn't seem frightening sitting on the ground. It looked like a long tube with wings and a tail. But still it was a plane. Images of the marketplace long ago in Syria started to creep into Abbas's mind.

He turned away from the window, put his headphones on and started a meditation. He focused on the voice and the gentle music. He stretched out his feet, feeling the muscles tighten and then relax. As long as he didn't look at the plane through the window, Abbas was okay.

"Ladies and gentlemen, WestJet Flight would like to start boarding Flight 702 to Toronto."

Abbas heard the voice above the music in his headphones. His heart thumped loudly.

"We'd also like to welcome the Grandview Eagles Soccer team. The boys are flying to Toronto to play in the Top Flight tournament," said the agent at the gate. "As a special treat we invite them to board first."

"You hear that, boys?" asked Coach T. "Get your stuff! It's time to go!"

13
WestJet Flight 702

The walk down the ramp seemed the longest distance Abbas had ever travelled.

"You're okay," whispered Dylan. "One foot in front of the other."

They reached the front door of the plane.

Abbas paused. "I'm not sure I can do it."

"Yes you can," said Claude. "Three more steps and you're on."

Abbas breathed deeply and moved forward. "One," he said. Everyone he cared about wanted him to get on that plane. He was not about to let them down.

"Two," said Dylan, from behind him as Abbas took another step.

"Three," said Claude. With that Abbas stepped over the gap, through the door and into the plane.

Abbas didn't remember much at all about the flight from Turkey to Canada. So he was surprised at what he saw. From the inside the plane didn't look much different from a long bus.

"You boys are in row twenty-eight, seats A, B and C," said a smiling flight attendant. "That's toward the back on your right."

Abbas clenched and unclenched his fist as they walked toward their row.

"Which seat do you want?" Claude asked Abbas. "The window?"

The last thing Abbas wanted was to look outside. "The middle if you're good with it."

They were. Claude took the window and Dylan sat in the aisle seat.

Abbas took out his iPod and put on his headphones. A familiar calming voice and gentle music filled his ears. Abbas shut his eyes and breathed deeply. As the minutes passed he started to feel calm. But then he felt a nudge in his ribs.

"You have to turn that off," Dylan said. "We are about to take off."

Abbas took off the headphones and listened as the flight attendant talked about what to do in the "unlikely event of an emergency."

"This isn't exactly helping," Abbas muttered.

The flight attendant took his seat as the pilot came on the intercom. "Welcome to WestJet Flight 702 to Toronto," she said as the plane lurched backward. Abbas's heart lurched along with it. "We'll be taking off in just a few minutes. Estimated flight time to Pearson International Airport is four and a half hours."

Abbas groaned. "That's like forever."

Claude patted him on his shoulder. "You'll be fine."

The plane's engines roared to life as it started to move forward.

"We'll be arriving at approximately 5:45 in the afternoon, Toronto time," the pilot continued. "Please feel free to use any personal devices you have, as long as they are switched to airplane mode. We'll be in the air soon. So sit back, relax and enjoy your flight."

Abbas put the headphones back on. Soon, the gentle sound of waves and a calming voice filled his ears. At that point he couldn't have cared less if the rest of the team heard it. He shut his eyes and started his muscle-relaxing exercises again.

Through the guided mediation he heard the engines grow as loud as thunder. He felt his body pressed back into the seat as the plane shot down the runway, gaining speed for takeoff.

Dylan and Claude each put a hand on Abbas's arm closest to them. Abbas was terrified. But knowing his two best friends were on either side of him made it better. Abbas's stomach seemed lift as the plane took off. As it gained altitude he felt his ears pop. *Breathe, breathe. You can do this.*

A few minutes later Abbas opened his eyes. Dylan and Claude gave him a thumbs up. He had done it! He was in the air. Now all he had to do was survive four hours and twenty minutes until he was back on the ground.

"Wow, is that a great view!" said Claude. "You should look."

"I'm fine," Abbas said.

"Come on, it is really cool. It can't hurt you."

Abbas hesitantly looked out the window. Claude was right. It was a great view. Vancouver spread our below them. To the north were the mountains. To the west was the Strait of Georgia and Vancouver Island.

"There's Stanley Park," said Claude. "And BC Place."

Abbas looked until the plane flew through clouds and the view disappeared. Then he shut his eyes again and listened to the music.

Abbas yawned. He had barely slept the night before. He was exhausted. *There's no way I can sleep*, he thought. But five minutes later he drifted off and fell deeply asleep. Abbas didn't wake up until four hours later when the plane began its descent.

"Abbas! You have to see this!" said Claude.

Abbas opened his eyes. "See what?" he asked.

"Toronto," Claude replied. "We're here."

Abbas couldn't believe it. The last thing he remembered was Vancouver far below him. Now it was Toronto he was looking at.

"Wow!" said Dylan. He leaned over Abbas to look out the window himself. "This place is huge!"

Vancouver was a big city but nothing compared to what they saw below. Buildings, roads and houses spread out from the shores of Lake Ontario, a lake that seemed almost as large as the Pacific Ocean.

"There's the CN Tower!" said Claude.

"And BMO Field!" said Abbas. "Where Toronto FC plays."

The pilot came onto the intercom. "We'll be on the ground shortly," she said as the plane banked to the left. "Thank you for flying WestJet."

Abbas breathed deeply as the plane descended. The buildings got larger and the airport closer and closer. Then he felt a bump as the wheels of the plane touched down. The engines roared, slowing down the plane. A few seconds later they were taxiing slowly toward the gate. Flight over.

He had done it!

"Okay, boys," said Coach T. "We're here!"

14
The Eagles Have Landed

"Welcome to Toronto," said a man as the team entered the arrivals area. "My name is Mathew Yang. I'm the organizer of Top Flight and a friend of Jon Lutz."

"Thank you for inviting us," Coach T said.

"It's my pleasure. I'm glad you can join us. There's a bus waiting for you outside. You're staying at the Chestnut Residence downtown. Chestnut used to be a hotel, but the University of Toronto uses it for student housing these days. After classes end for the summer they rent it out to tourists or anyone visiting the city."

"This is better than a school bus," Junior said. The bus the team boarded was a luxury coach.

"You're our guests and we want you to feel at home," Mathew said. "The driver will take you to Chestnut once he drops me off at my car. You'll be there in forty-five minutes or so. Traffic is a little heavy this time of day. I've organized pizza for dinner. There is a cafeteria in the residence and you guys will eat there most of the time. But it will be closed by the time you arrive tonight."

"Pizza is fine by us!" said Claude. "Thank you very much."

"Mathew, how do you know Jon Lutz?" Coach T asked.

"We're connected through business . . . and friendship," Mathew answered. "I'm the owner and president of Electro Video Games. Have you heard of our stores? We sell a lot of EA games."

"Electro is my favourite store in the universe," said Dylan.

The feeling was shared by the other boys on the team. "Jon inspired me to start a Canada Scores Chapter here in Toronto. When he told me about your team I just knew we had to have you play in our tournament. There are sixteen boys teams and sixteen girls teams. They make up East and West Divisions of eight teams each for both boys and girls. We put you in the boys West Division. You're the most western team we've ever had!"

"When do we play?" Junior asked.

"Your first game tomorrow is at noon against the Brampton Selects," Mathew said before he stepped off the bus. "The opening ceremony is ten o'clock tomorrow. That's seven in the morning Vancouver time. So I suggest you go to bed early. Good luck!"

The door shut and the bus pulled away. "You heard him," said Coach T. "We'll check in, have dinner and then it's back to your rooms for nine o'clock."

"Nine?" Mo groaned. "That's six o'clock our time. My sister doesn't even have to go to bed that early. And she's in grade one!"

"Your sister isn't playing the Brampton Selects tomorrow. I don't think you want to come all this way to lose your first game because you're tired."

The bus travelled along the busiest road Abbas had ever seen. "Welcome to Highway 427, boys," said the driver, as the bus inched along.

The Eagles didn't mind the traffic. They were too busy taking in the sights.

"We're almost at Chestnut Residences," said the driver as the bus turned onto Chestnut Street. "Nathan Phillips Square and City Hall are to the south, as is the CN Tower and the waterfront. The University and Varsity Stadium are to the north. You are right in the centre of everything."

The boys thanked the driver. They unloaded their cases, walked up to a tall, square building and entered through the large glass doors.

"Welcome," said a young man at the front desk. "We have seven rooms for you on the twenty-second floor."

Coach T had his own room while the players doubled up. "Steven and Carlos are in 2201," said Coach T as they reached their floor. "Alvin and Jun are next door and Junior and Mo are across the hall."

Abbas and Claude were roommates in 2209.

"What a great view!" said Claude, pulling back the curtains. Their room faced Lake Ontario, and they could see City Hall and the CN Tower.

"There is a common room down the hall," Coach T said from the hallway. "Pizza will be here in twenty minutes. Unpack and then come and get some food."

"Great! I'm starving," said Claude.

"Give me just a minute," Abbas said. Abbas didn't have a phone. But his iPod was loaded with a ton of social media apps.

Abbas logged into the Chestnut Wi-Fi and sent a quick message to his mom, letting her know he'd made it okay. Then he texted Victor.

In Toronto.

It didn't take Victor long to answer.

Where u staying?

Some place called Chestnut. U?

Home. We R driving in TAM for opening ceremony

CUITM Gotta eat pizza. Starving!

LOL. CU

"You ready?" Claude asked Abbas. "If we don't hurry Mo will eat everything."

Abbas put away his iPod. "I was just saying hello to my friend Victor."

The boys gathered in the common room. Their mouths watered at the smell and sight of the pizza waiting for them on the table. And they wasted no time digging in.

"This is really tasty," said Junior. He was working on his third piece of cheese pizza.

"Don't go too crazy," Coach T said. "I don't want you having tummy aches tomorrow morning for the game."

"Don't you worry about us," Steven laughed. "We can handle our pizza."

Coach T looked at his watch. "You can handle going to bed as well. It's 8:45 right now. Fifteen minutes from now I want you in your rooms. Watch TV, talk for a bit if you want, but I want you all asleep by ten."

"Ten p.m. here is like lunchtime back in Vancouver, Coach," William said. Then, despite himself, he yawned.

"Maybe, but Claude's not the only one who gets feelings," said Coach T. "I have a feeling most of you will be fast asleep within half an hour."

The boys were tired. Abbas had spent most of the flight asleep, but he could hardly keep his eyes open.

"Good night, Claude," Abbas said. He climbed into his bed. "Thanks for your help. I don't think I would have been able to fly here without you and the guys."

"You're welcome," Claude replied. "I have a feeling it will be worth it. Tomorrow is going to be a great day, I just know it."

15
Top Flight Begins

"Ladies and gentlemen, the Brampton Selects!"

Abbas and the rest of the Eagles could hear the crowd cheer loudly. They were standing anxiously in the tunnels under the stands of Varsity Stadium.

The tunnel ahead and behind them was stuffed with soccer players. They all were waiting their turn to march onto the field in alphabetical order, just like the teams in the Olympic opening ceremony.

A young girl and boy, both about ten years old, stood in front of Abbas. They carried a large green and gold banner that read *Grandview Eagles*.

"The Etobicoke Strikers will be called next," said a tournament marshal. "Grandview, you'll be after them. You guys look great, by the way. Those track suits are very sharp."

"It's all about deportment," said Claude. The boys shuffled toward the tunnel exit as the two teams in front of them walked out.

Then it was their turn.

Top Flight Begins

"A special Top Flight welcome for the Grandview Eagles from Burnaby, British Columbia!" said the announcer. He was standing on a stage set up at the far end of the stadium, along with other people Abbas guessed were VIPs.

With their banner leading the way, the Eagles stepped out onto the pitch. The stands in Varsity Stadium were full, with more than five thousand people cheering the teams as they entered.

Varsity Stadium was much smaller than BC Place, where Abbas and the Vancouver Herons had played in the final game against Victor's team. But it was exciting to be here, maybe even more exciting than the All-Syrian tournament. While it had been an honour to play for the Herons, there was something very meaningful about this tournament with his school friends, boys who meant the world to him.

"Hall United!" said the announcer next. That was Victor's team! They must have been right next to each other in the tunnel. But it had been so tightly packed Abbas hadn't seen his friend.

Right behind his team's banner walked Victor. Victor saw Abbas and gave him a smile as his team lined up next to Grandview.

For the next fifteen minutes the rest of the teams, boys and girls alike, walked proudly out into the stadium. "Willowdale FC!" said the announcer as the very last team stepped onto the turf surface of Varsity Stadium.

Golden Game

"Please rise for the singing of our national anthem." As one, the fans in the stands stood up as "O Canada" played over the loudspeakers. Varsity Stadium filled with the sound of thousands of people singing.

Abbas put his hand over his heart and joined them. *It's pretty amazing*, he thought, looking around the stadium. So many people from all over the world were there, standing alongside native-born Canadians, all singing the anthem of their shared country. He was really glad he had found the courage to get on that plane.

The song ended, the fans took their seats and there were some speeches. A Member of Parliament spoke, followed by a Member of the Provincial Parliament, the Mayor of Toronto and the Chancellor of the University of Toronto.

They all said nice things, and each speech was greeted with polite applause. Then a familiar face came up to the microphone. "My name is Mathew Yang, the tournament organizer," the man said. "And it's time to play soccer!"

The crowd cheered at that. Speeches were fine, but everyone knew why they were all there!

"Teams, you will be playing at five different fields," Mathew explained. "Varsity Stadium, the two fields at the U of T back campus, as well as Jesse Ketchum and Central Technical Schools. The really great thing about Central Tech is that they have a brand new turf field and it is covered by a dome!"

"Wow!" Abbas said to Dylan. "Just like BC Place?"

"Although it doesn't seat fifty thousand people," Dylan replied.

"Your coaches have been given today's schedule," continued Mathew. "Tomorrow's matches will be posted at Tournament Headquarters at the main entrance of Varsity Stadium by five each day. Good luck! Let the games begin!"

"We play Brampton on Field 1 at Back Campus," said Coach T.

There were shuttle buses to take the players to their game sites. But Coach T decided they would walk the ten minutes or so.

"Some of these building look more like castles than a school," Junior said. Vancouver was a very young city and while it did have some older buildings, the University of Toronto campus looked like it had been there since the Middle Ages.

"Maybe one day I'll come and study here," said Michael.

"Of course you will," said Coach T. "You can do anything you dream of. All of you can."

The buildings that surrounded the part of the university called Back Campus were old, but the beautiful turf fields were very new.

"Here we are, boys," Coach T said. "Field 1. It's 11:30. Get warmed up. We play in thirty minutes."

Claude led the boys out onto the field to stretch. Abbas looked anxiously at the Brampton players, kicking balls around at the other end of the field.

"They look pretty good," said Mo. "And pretty big."

It was hard for Abbas to disagree. Dressed in their red and blue uniforms the Brampton players were as big as the Burnaby Creek Bulldogs.

"This is real, isn't it?" Junior said. The weeks leading up to the tournament had been exciting, and the opening ceremonies fun as well. But now they were here, more than halfway across the country, playing in the biggest tournament of their lives.

"Very real," Claude said.

"I'm so nervous I don't think I can feel my toes!" Carlos said.

Abbas looked at his teammates, his friends. He could see their nerves, could almost feel them. He was worried. It felt like Brampton was already beating them and the game hadn't even started yet.

"Huddle up," Abbas said. "I had to learn to control my fear to get on the plane. We can do the same thing now. My friend Haval taught me a few tricks to relax. So shut your eyes, breathe deeply and do what I do."

Abbas was on edge, but after five minutes of deep breathing and stretching his muscles he felt better. He was pleased to see that Claude and the rest of the boys looked less stressed as well, as they ran a few drills and then took turns taking shots on Michael.

"Okay, boys," the ref said, looking at his watch. "Captains, come here please for the coin toss."

Claude walked to the centre of the field where he was joined by a tall South Asian boy who captained the Brampton team. They shook hands.

"We play two thirty-minute halves," said the ref. "If the game is tied after that, we move right into a five minute sudden-death overtime. You know what sudden death means?"

"Golden goal." Claude smiled as he spoke. The Eagles had been there before. But this time it would be for bigger stakes than they could ever have imagined.

"Correct. If the score is still tied after that, we move into penalty kicks. The winner moves to the quarter-finals. You call the coin toss, Brampton."

"Heads," the Brampton player said as the ref tossed a loonie high into the air.

"Heads it is," the ref said as the coin hit the turf. "Brampton kicks off."

Coach T called the Eagles in for a huddle. "Play your best and I will be proud of you, win or lose."

"Hands in," said Claude.

"Play hard," he said beginning their favourite cheer.

"Play safe," the boys shouted. "Play fair! Go Eagles!"

The referee blew his whistle and the boys walked out onto the field.

16
The Brampton Selects

Brampton scored five minutes into the game. A defender sent the ball up the left-hand side of the field with a beautiful long pass. A midfielder took the pass and in one graceful movement lobbed it into the crease. The two Brampton strikers rushed after it, beating Mo and William, leaving only Alvin between the attackers and Michael.

The ball bounced high and hard on the turf field. A tall Brampton striker leaped into the air and directed the ball into the bottom left corner of the net with his head. Michael dove, but just missed the ball.

The score was 1–0, Brampton.

"Settle down, boys," encouraged Coach T from the sidelines. "Play your game. You have lots of time."

The Eagles were nervous. They looked tense, like they weren't enjoying playing soccer at all.

Claude called a quick huddle. "Remember that final game against Regent Heights?" he asked.

"Of course," Dylan said.

"Who did everyone expect to win that game?"

"Regent, of course," said Jake. "They were the favourites. Nobody thought we could beat them."

"Except us," Claude corrected him. "It's just like that now, except now we aren't just playing for ourselves. We're representing our school, our city, even our province. So let's get out there and show them what the Grandview Eagles can do!"

Maybe it was the speech or maybe the boys had worked out their nerves. When Abbas took the kick-off and sent the ball back to Junior, the team seemed to settle down.

Junior took the ball and ran up the middle of the field with Mo and Abdul in support. As he did a large Brampton midfielder with long blond hair closed in on him. Junior faked a pass to Mo. The midfielder fell for it and Junior deked past.

Junior sent the ball to Abdul. One touch later Abdul kicked it along the right side of the field to Abbas. Dylan kept up on the left side, while Claude dropped back in support.

Five metres out of the Brampton crease, and with two Brampton defenders closing in, Dylan passed the ball to Claude. Claude side-stepped a defender. At the top of the crease, he booted the ball as hard as he could.

It looked as if the ball was heading straight, but then it suddenly curved to the right. The Brampton goalie tried to adjust. He leaped desperately, but it was too late.

The ball slammed into the back of the net.

Brampton: 1, Grandview: 1.

The boys hugged Claude as they made their way back to the centre of the field.

"See?" Claude said. "These guys aren't unbeatable."

There were ten minutes left in the first half of the game. Even though the score was tied, the Eagles carried most of the play. They even came close to taking the lead on a great free kick by Dylan that rattled off the goalpost to the goalie's left.

The ref blew the whistle. The Grandview Eagles walked to the sideline with smiles on their faces.

"Great job!" said Coach T.

After a five-minute break the second half began. This time Grandview kicked off.

Brampton had expected to win the game easily. At the start of the game the Brampton players had looked confident. They didn't anymore. Being tied at the half with a team of younger kids from across the country was not in their plans.

A few minutes later, Brampton came close to scoring the go-ahead goal. They earned a corner kick after William stretched out his foot to break up a pass and sent the ball out of bounds.

When the Brampton player took the corner kick, the ball curved, heading straight to the top corner of the net. Michael jumped and managed to get enough of his fingertips on the ball to send it to the corner. Jake collected it and kicked it safely down the field.

For the next twenty minutes the play went back and forth, with no quality chances for either team. It looked like the game could go into extra time, or maybe even penalty kicks.

Then Grandview got a lucky break.

"Here!" shouted Dylan. Abdul and a Brampton midfielder were fighting for the ball at centre field. Abdul won it and sent the ball high toward Dylan.

Dylan was too far up to get any support, and so he took it himself, heading right toward the Brampton net. Two defenders rushed toward him, cutting off the angle.

At the top of the crease, with nowhere to go and no one to pass to, Dylan booted the ball as hard as he could. He was hoping to send it between the defenders, but the ball took a crazy bounce and smacked into the outstretched arm of another defender standing a metre or so away.

Tweet! The referee pointed to the penalty spot.

The Brampton players looked stunned.

"Accidental!" the Brampton coach shouted. But the referee was having none of it. Penalty shot for Grandview.

"Abbas, take it," said Coach T.

Abbas felt his heart race. The game was almost over. Five minutes at most remained. This was not a golden goal, but it was a golden chance.

Abbas picked up the ball and placed it at the penalty spot. The Brampton goalkeeper stood on his line. He waved his hands in the air trying to distract Abbas.

The Brampton goalie wasn't as tall as Majok from the Bulldogs, but he was big enough to fill the net. On the sidelines people yelled. The fans watching the game, all Brampton supporters, hollered and jeered at Abbas to miss.

With a sharp kick Abbas sent the ball into the air. It was low, not more than a metre above the ground. The ball was easily saveable if the goalie guessed correctly.

Abbas's shot went right as the goalkeeper moved to his left. He could do nothing as the ball sailed into the net.

Grandview: 2, Brampton: 1.

The Eagles swarmed Abbas while a Brampton player picked up the ball and hurried to the middle of the field. A minute, maybe two, was left in the game.

Brampton kicked off, sending every player, including their goalkeeper, toward Michael and the Grandview net.

On defence, Jun slid toward an approaching Brampton midfielder. Jun's foot connected with the ball, sending it to Steven who booted it down the field as far as he could.

A Brampton defender ran desperately back. The rest of the players on both teams looked at the ref.

Blow the whistle, blow the whistle, Abbas whispered under his breath.

Tweet! It was as if the referee read his mind. The game ended. Grandview erupted in cheers. Some Brampton players stood in shock while their coach hung his head in disbelief.

"Don't forget your sportsmanship," Coach T reminded his players.

The Eagles lined up and shook the hands of the Brampton players, coach and finally the referees.

"Way to go, Abbas!" said Claude, slapping his friend on the back.

"Good thing you overcame your fear of flights!" said Dylan. "One down, three to go!"

17
Old Friends

"Did you guys win your game?" Victor asked.

"2–1 against Brampton. You?" Hall United had played at Jesse Ketchum School that afternoon. It was all Abbas could do to wait to Facetime his friend.

"4–0 over Markham."

"That's great!" Abbas said. "We're both in the quarterfinals."

"With a bit of luck we'll face each other in the finals again."

"You beat me in my hometown. It will be my turn to return the favour in yours."

Victor laughed. "Don't worry. The best team will win."

"Of course," Abbas said. "And that will be the Grandview Eagles."

"We'll see," Victor said. "What are you doing tonight?"

"We're going back to Chestnut now and then we're going up the CN Tower. Coach T says we can't come all the way to Toronto and not go up the CN Tower."

"Your coach is right. The view from up there is amazing. After that can you go out for dinner with my family? My mom and dad really want to see you."

Abbas was thrilled at the invitation. "I'll have to ask Coach T but I'm sure it will be all right."

"Good. Call me after you get back from the CN Tower."

Abbas went to find Coach T. He was surprised to find that Coach T had been expecting the question.

"Your mom said you would ask," said Coach T. "It's fine with me. But stay close and be back by eight. I don't yet know who or when we play tomorrow, and the first game starts at nine o'clock. I want you rested. In the meantime round up the guys. We are going sightseeing."

⚽ ⚽ ⚽

"You have to be kidding me. There is no way I'm going up there." Alvin stood at the base of the CN Tower, staring up into the sky. "I'm scared of heights, remember?"

"I'm scared of planes. But I flew here." Abbas wasn't going to be the only member of the Eagles to overcome his fear on this trip.

"Okay," said Alvin reluctantly. "But don't expect me to look down when we get to the top."

It was a fair deal, but one Alvin regretted almost as

soon as he stepped into the elevator. The elevator walls were made of glass. "You have to be kidding me," he said again, shutting his eyes.

Abbas's stomach lurched as the elevator started upwards. It moved far faster than any he'd been in before. Before him the city of Toronto spread out. The view got better and better the higher they climbed.

Soon the elevator stopped.

"Check this out," said Coach T. "Look below you, Alvin." A section of the floor was made of glass. They could see all the way to the ground, some three hundred metres below.

"No way!" said Alvin as the other boys stepped off the regular floor and onto the glass.

The view was incredible. Lake Ontario looked as big as a sea. They were above even the tallest skyscrapers. Abbas felt he could see almost all the way home to Burnaby.

After half an hour the boys had seen enough. They had eaten lunch at Chestnut but that had seemed ages before. It was almost five and time to get back for dinner. Their next match would be posted as well, and Coach T was anxious to find out the details.

As soon as Abbas got back to his room he Facetimed Victor. "I'm allowed to go with you guys for dinner. What time?"

"Meet me in the lobby in twenty minutes," Victor said.

Old Friends

☻ ☻ ☻

Abbas watched as Victor, his mom, his dad and his little brother walked through the front doors of Chestnut.

"Abbas!" Victor's mom cried. "You look so big!"

"Thanks." Abbas was a little embarrassed at the attention. Victor's mom ran over to him and hugged him tightly. When she was done Victor's dad did the same thing. Both had tears in their eyes.

"Hi," said Victor's little brother in English. He shook Abbas's hand shyly. "I'm Gabriel."

"I think I remember you. I was younger than you when I left Syria. You were just a little baby then."

Once he saw their faces Abbas remembered Victor's mom and dad, even though it had been years. Their families had been as close as families could be without being related after all.

"A pleasure to meet you," said Coach T. He had been waiting in the lobby with Abbas.

"And you." Victor's dad shook Coach T's hand. Victor's mom put her hand to her heart in a greeting. "Thank you for allowing Abbas to come to dinner with us. We are going to Aleppo's. They have the best kebab in town."

Victor's mom shot her husband a look.

"Sorry, I mean second best kebab in town." He grinned. "My wife makes the best, of course. We would have liked to have taken Abbas to our home in Scarborough but the traffic this time of day is crazy. Would you like to come to the restaurant as well, Coach Whitebear?"

Abbas wasn't surprised Coach T got an invitation. He knew Syrians to be very hospitable people.

"Thank you, but I need to stay with the rest of the boys," said Coach T.

"I understand," said Victor's dad. "In that case we will send Abbas back with some food. May I have your cell number to let you know when we are bringing him back?"

Coach T gave him the number and Victor's dad put it in his contacts. Then they all walked out of Chestnut and into the warm evening air.

"I told you it was close," said Victor's dad as they walked down Elm Street just five minutes later. Aleppo's was a small place, in between a Japanese and Chinese restaurant.

They were greeted warmly in Arabic by the owner of the restaurant. He showed them to a table in the back.

"I cannot believe we are seeing each other again," beamed Victor's mom. "When we all fled Syria I never thought our families would meet again!"

"And to be in a country like Canada," said Victor's dad. "It is remarkable."

Abbas thought so too. As Victor and his parents talked they brought back memories of things Abbas had long forgotten. He recalled places they'd visited, old friends of good times.

The food was even better than Victor's dad had promised. Plates of naan, tabbouleh, kebab and kibbeh appeared before them. Victor, Gabriel and Abbas drank water while Victor's mom and dad enjoyed cups of strong Syrian coffee with the restaurant owner. It turned out he knew one of Abbas's uncles back home. It was a very small world.

It was a magical evening full of good memories, laughs and stories. It ended far too soon.

"Look at the time!" said Victor's mom. "We have kept Abbas out too long. His coach will be getting worried. Besides, both of you boys have important games tomorrow."

Victor's dad paid the bill and sent Coach T a quick text. When they left the restaurant it was dark, and the night was getting cool. "Thank you so much," Abbas said. "It was a great night! I hope you all can come and see my mom in Burnaby someday. She talks about you all the time."

"We would love that, too," Victor's dad replied as they reached the front door of the Chestnut Residence. Abbas saw Coach T waiting outside for him, a smile on the coach's face.

"Thank you for letting Abbas go with us," said Victor's dad, giving Coach T a plastic bag full of lamb kebab and naan. "Second best kebab in town, as promised."

"You didn't have to do this but thank you," Coach T said. "It smells delicious. How was Abbas, by the way?"

"He is a very good boy," Victor's mom said, hugging Abbas again, to his embarrassment.

"You play Mississauga tomorrow, right?" Victor asked. "We play Richmond Hill. Our game starts half an hour before yours. I will try to catch the end of yours."

As they waved goodbye to the Bayazids, Coach T said to Abbas, "You had a good time I can tell."

"The best," said Abbas. The only thing now that could make the trip any better would be meeting Victor's team in the final. And being on the winning team this time.

18
The Mississauga Mustangs

"How did Mississauga do yesterday?" asked Abbas. Their shuttle bus came to a stop at Jesse Ketchum School, an old brick building that looked much larger than Burnaby Creek Secondary.

"They beat Milton FC in penalties," Coach T said. "It was a tough game. We have to hope they'll be tired."

The Mississauga Mustangs, in their light blue uniforms, were kicking the ball around. They didn't seem tired. And they didn't play tired when the game began ten minutes later.

The Mustangs were big. But Grandview was full of confidence and it showed, even after an early scare when a Mississauga player sent a long shot on net that Michael easily handled. After that the Eagles settled down and dominated the play.

"I'm open!" shouted Dylan a few plays later. Mo saw him flash down the wing and sent him the ball. Claude followed closely behind. Dylan faked right and back-passed the ball to Claude. He cheered as Claude dribbled past a defender and blasted the ball into the net. Five minutes in. Grandview: 1, Mississauga: 0.

"Maybe they *are* tired," said Steven, standing on the sideline. He was starting as a sub.

"And down two of their best players," replied Coach T. He pointed at two unhappy-looking Mississauga players sitting on the bench in their track suits, watching the game. "Their best striker sprained his ankle. The other one got a red card yesterday. He is suspended for this game."

As the game went on, Mississauga got frustrated. The few times they took the ball they ended up losing it to the quick feet of Jun, Abdul or Claude.

Then a fight nearly broke out toward the end of the half. With the score still 1–0, Abbas took a pass from Claude and moved up the field. He was ten metres across centre when out of the corner of his eye he saw a blue flash.

The next thing he knew, Abbas was lying on the turf, a sharp pain burning his calf.

Tweet! went the ref's whistle.

"That was on purpose!" shouted Dylan. He ran over to Abbas and got into the face of Mississauga's number 14 who had raked Abbas's calf with his cleats. Number 14 was a short boy who reminded Dylan of Liam, the rat-faced kid from Regent Heights.

"What are you going to do about it?" 14 sneered, stepping toward Dylan and shoving him in the chest.

"Walk away," said Claude. He wrapped his arms around Dylan and pulled him away before he could shove the player back.

Tweet! The ref reached into his pocket, pulled out a red card and waved it.

"No way!" 14 shouted. But even his coach saw how unsportsmanlike his player had been.

"I'm sorry about that," the coach said to Abbas, stepping onto the field to get number 14. "Lucas isn't usually like that. It's been a bad tournament for us so far."

Jun and William helped Abbas to his feet.

"Are you okay?" the ref asked. "Do you need to be subbed off?"

Abbas walked off the pain. "I'm fine. Let's play."

Mississauga played hard. But down one goal and one more player, they were unable to stop the Eagles. Five minutes later Grandview had scored again on a point-blank blast from Abdul.

Grandview: 2, Mississauga: 0.

Abbas hobbled off the field when the half-time whistle blew.

"Abbas, you're sitting off the second half," said Coach T. "Claude, move up to striker. Carlos, take midfield. Get warmed up."

"You bet," Carlos said, taking off his track suit.

"Coach! I'm fine," Abbas protested.

"We're up two-nil against a tired team with ten players. If we can't beat them without you then we are in trouble. Rest your leg. With a bit of luck we will be in the semi-finals tomorrow. We'll need you more then."

Abbas didn't like sitting out but he saw that Coach T was right. He limped to the bench. There he put on his track suit top and wrapped an icepack onto his bruised calf.

Five minutes into the second half Steven scored. As a fullback, he didn't score very much. But this time he placed a beautiful kick over the goalie's head, much to the delight of the Eagles.

From the bench Abbas saw a look on the Mustangs player's face he recognized. Defeat. Shorthanded, down by three goals and with some of their best players on the bench, Mississauga was beaten and they knew it.

Abbas had been there. His first game with the Eagles against Regent Heights last season. The Eagles on the field saw the same thing that Abbas did. Unlike Dylan's old school they didn't try take advantage of it.

The Eagles took their feet off the gas. Although they could have easily scored three or four more goals they didn't put the ball in the net again. The final whistle blew.

Grandview: 3, Mississauga: 0.

"I'm really sorry," said number 14 to Abbas as they shook hands. "I was just upset at how we were playing."

"It's okay," Abbas told him. "I know how it feels."

"Good luck in the semi-finals," the Mississauga

coach told Coach T. "You guys have class. You could have run up the score but you didn't. I appreciate that."

"Hey, Abbas!" a voice called out. Abbas turned to see Victor. "Way to go! You guys made the Western finals!"

"I sat the last half of the game though," Abbas said. He showed Victor his bruised calf. "Took a bad tackle. How did your team do?"

Victor's team had started their game at Varsity thirty minutes before the Eagles kicked off.

"We won 2-1 against Richmond Hill. We are in the semis too. You never know, maybe we'll meet in the final!"

"What are you doing here?" Abbas asked.

"I told my mom I wanted to hang out with you for a bit, if you want," Victor said. "I'll take the TTC back to Scarborough Centre later."

Coach T gave Abbas permission and he and Victor went to an ice cream shop on University Avenue. It was a warm day and the two friends enjoyed their cones and the sun on their faces.

"This is pretty special isn't it?" Victor said.

"What is?" Abbas asked, between licks of his chocolate ice cream.

"For us to be here in Canada, playing soccer after all the things that happened to us back home. We are very lucky."

"We are. I nearly didn't make it," Abbas confided.

"What do you mean?" Victor asked.

"To Toronto. It was having to fly, to get on a plane. It was so hard. When I was little there was a bombing back home, in the . . ."

"Market." Victor finished the sentence for him. "Right before your family left for Turkey. I remember my mom telling me."

"When I thought of getting on a plane all I could picture was the bomber flying over us. The noise, the flames, the crying. It's still there. It always will be. But I learned to manage it." Abbas paused before asking, "How often do you think of Syria?"

"Every day. I still have family back there. My mom has a sister. We haven't heard from her or her kids in weeks. My mom's worried."

Abbas fell silent. He had uncles, aunts and cousins who had gone missing as well. They could be anywhere: Syria, Turkey, Jordan. They could even be . . .

Abbas shivered. He didn't like to think about the end of that sentence. "When do you think there will be peace?"

Victor shrugged. "Soon, I hope, but the war has been going on for so long. It seems it will never end."

They talked about friends, about family and their old homes. It was hard for Abbas to talk about these things to anyone else, but with Victor the words came easily.

Victor *got it.*

Some of his friends like Claude had been refugees as well. But with Victor it was different. Abbas and Victor spoke the same language, had watched the same TV shows as kids, had lived in the same places.

Victor's phone beeped. "That's my mom," he said. "I have to get home. Come on, I'll walk with you to St. Patrick subway station. It's really close to Chestnut."

Abbas stood up and limped away from the patio.

"How's your leg feeling?" Victor asked.

"It should be okay for tomorrow," Abbas told him.

"I hope so," Victor grinned, "because if we do meet in the final I wouldn't want you to use it as an excuse!"

19
Yorkdale FC

Grandview and Yorkdale FC stepped off the pitch for half-time to a huge round of applause. Varsity Stadium was more than half-full. The three thousand fans reminded the Eagles again that Top Flight was a very big deal.

"Well done!" beamed Coach T. "This is the best soccer I've ever seen you play!"

The score was 0–0. Michael and the Yorkdale goalkeeper each had made several remarkable saves, and the pace of the first half had been fast and furious.

Yorkdale had won Top Flight the year before and were fielding a strong team again. But some people in the stands were cheering for Grandview. The Eagles had won over many people with their great soccer. They were also special because of the great distance the team had travelled. And the story of how they won the Burnaby championship had been posted on the Top Flight website.

"I feel like we're playing against the Vancouver Whitecaps!" moaned Abdul, lying down on the turf.

"Are you kidding? More like Barcelona!" said Claude, dropping to the ground next to him. The midfielders on both teams had been running almost nonstop since the game began.

"Hang in there, boys," Coach T said. "One goal is all it will take to win this game. I can't believe how well you've done!"

The Grandview Eagles from south Burnaby were in the semi-finals. They were just one goal away from winning the Western Division and playing Hall United in the championship the next afternoon.

"Go Grandview!" Abbas heard Victor and the rest of his team cheer from the stands. The Eagles had watched Hall United win their semi-final 3–2 against the Don Valley All-Stars, right before they took the field at Varsity Stadium themselves.

Tweet! The whistle blew to start the second half.

Abbas took another long drink from his water bottle. He walked out onto the field beside Dylan and Claude. His calf was bruised and looked bad, and it had been stiff earlier. But now it felt okay.

"They look as tired as we do," said Claude. "That's a good sign." The black and red striped shirts of the Yorkdale players were stained with sweat.

The second half was very defensive. Both teams were tired. All of them knew that one mistake could cost their team the game. The teams split possession equally, with most of the game played in the centre of the field.

Claude and a Yorkdale striker were fighting for a loose ball.

"Claude!" shouted Dylan suddenly.

Claude came up with the ball and kicked it toward Dylan.

With Abbas beside him, Dylan dribbled toward the Yorkdale goal. Three fullbacks rushed out to meet him, cutting off any hope of a good shot.

Dylan tapped the ball toward Abbas. Abbas was just as far out as Dylan was. But at least Abbas had a clear shot. When Abbas was twenty yards from the goal a fullback sprinted toward him.

Abbas knew that if the game had just started and if his leg wasn't throbbing, he could have beat the fullback. Instead, Abbas leaned into the ball and kicked with all his strength. It was a low-percentage shot but it was the best he could do. The Yorkdale goalkeeper positioned himself in the net and caught the ball squarely in front of his chest.

Abbas's kick was the best chance either team had for the rest of the half. For the first time since Top Flight began, Grandview ended regulation time tied.

"Looks like it's Golden Goal time," said Coach T as the players huddled around him.

"You up for being the hero again?" Coach T asked Dylan.

"I don't care who scores," Dylan replied. "Just as long as they're wearing gold and green, not black and red!"

"Okay, guys," said Claude. "Listen up. I have an idea." He explained his plan in a quiet voice as his teammates leaned in.

Grandview was lucky enough to win the toss to start extra time. Claude's plan needed them to get control of the ball as soon as possible.

"Now!" Claude shouted once Dylan passed him the ball.

Usually teams played very cautiously to start extra time. Instead every Eagles player, except for three fullbacks, sprinted up the field. It caught Yorkdale by complete surprise. Claude looked for a target. He saw Junior rushing up the left side, with no Yorkdale players within fifteen metres of him. Claude expertly fed him the ball.

Junior looked to the right. Dylan, Abbas, Mo and Abdul were rushing forward, chased by a handful of Yorkdale players.

"Dylan!" shouted Junior. Dylan took the pass. He sent the ball to Mo, who was now at the top of the crease. There was only one Yorkdale fullback between Mo and the net.

With a grunt Mo kicked, sending a terrific shot at the goal. It went high and to the right. The Yorkdale goalie jumped, stretching his hand out as far as he could. Abbas watched the whole thing in what seemed to be slow motion.

The ball flew closer and closer to the goal line. The goalie flew closer and closer to the ball. A fingertip of the goalkeeper's hand hit the ball. Instead of going in, the ball deflected up and over the net.

Mo covered his face with his hands. The ball wasn't just stopped. Mo had been robbed of a sure goal by the best save they'd ever seen.

Tweet! The ref pointed to the corner arc to the right of the goal.

"Good thing we've been practising our corners," Claude said. "Three minutes to go until penalty kicks. I don't think any of us want to see what else this goalie can do in a shootout!"

Claude took the kick. Dylan, Abbas, Mo and Abdul took their spots in front of the goal.

Timing, watch your timing, Abbas told himself.

The whistle blew. Claude kicked a high arcing pass across the face of the goal. The ball was too high for Dylan and Mo. It sailed over their heads and dropped toward Abbas to the left of the goal.

Abbas was surrounded by a sea of red and black jerseys but he hardly noticed them. All his attention was on the ball, getting closer and closer.

Eyes open. On the forehead.

With the ball just a couple of metres away Abbas bent his knees, ignoring the pain in his bruised calf. With his eyes open he jumped higher than he'd ever jumped before. He met the ball with his forehead at the top of his leap.

Abbas sent the ball down hard and to the left. There

was a gap of half a metre between the goalie and the goal post. The Yorkdale goalkeeper lunged.

The ball hit the turf right in front of the goal line. It bounced up and over the goalie's foot. It crossed the line and rolled into the back netting. The crowd roared.

Grandview: 1, Yorkdale: 0. The Eagles were off to the finals!

20
The Finals Begin

Varsity Stadium was packed for the two championship games. The girls played first, with Kingston Road FC representing the Girls Eastern Division against the Western Division finalists Bloor United. The girls teams were marched in, their banners blowing proudly in front of them.

"And please welcome the boys finalists!" announced Mathew Yang. He pointed to the stands where Hall United and Grandview were sitting next to each other.

"In my wildest dreams I didn't expect this," said Victor. "I feel bad for you, though. You're going to lose to me twice in less than two months!"

Abbas grinned. "We'll see about that."

He looked around the stadium. It was standing room only as far as he could tell. "I wish my mom could see this," Abbas said.

"She will," Coach T replied. "The organizers are broadcasting the games online. I sent the link to Ms. Bhullar and she is showing the game in the Grandview gym. The entire school is going to watch it. So are your parents."

The boys broke out into huge smiles.

"Hear that, guys?" Claude said. "We're playing soccer on TV, just like Manchester United!"

"They're good," said Dylan as the girls' final got underway.

The crowd cheered as Bloor United scored on a great corner kick.

"She has a better kick than you, Claude!" laughed Jun.

"Time to get warmed up," said Coach T when the half-time whistle blew.

Hall United's coach started leading his team to the change rooms under the stadium.

"See you on the field, Abbas," Victor said as Abbas waved and entered the Grandview change room.

"I couldn't be prouder of you all than I am right now," said Coach T as Claude led them in their warmup stretches. "Win or lose, you have done an amazing job. I am proud to have been your coach."

Grandview walked out of the change room. They could hear the cheering in the stadium.

"Who won the girl's game?" Coach T asked.

"Bloor 2–1," the tournament marshal said.

"That's a good sign," said Claude. "West Division

girls are champs. Now it's up to us. After all, we are the most western team they've ever had!"

Grandview lined up with Hall United by the tunnel exit.

"You ready?" Victor asked.

"As ready as I'm going to be," Abbas replied.

The crowd cheered as the marshal marched them out onto the field. Abbas thought the support seemed almost equal between Grandview and Hall United.

With Victor leading them, Hall United came over to shake hands. Beside Victor was a boy with his right arm in a sling.

"Abbas, I want you to meet Ozzie," Victor said. "He's our other goalie but he can't play right now."

"Sprained my wrist warming up for the tournament," Ozzie said. "Lucky for you guys. I'm a much better goalie than Victor!"

Abbas could tell by the laughter they shared what close friends Victor and Ozzie were.

While Grandview had players from half a dozen countries, Abbas could see that the players on Hall United were either Syrian like Victor or Nigerian like Ozzie. The only other players were a blond boy named Dylan and a Welsh kid named Owen.

"What are the odds of this?" the two Dylans laughed as they shook hands.

One by one the Hall United players introduced themselves: Ade, Muhammad, Hassan, Tarek, Sunny,

The Finals Begin

Sam, Peter and Riad. Abbas was happy to meet Victor's school team. He could tell that, just like Abbas, Victor loved playing with his best friends, the guys he saw every day. And both of them would really love to win playing for these teams.

Then both teams turned to the ref as he said, "Captains, may I see you for the coin toss, please?"

Claude started to walk toward the ref. Then he stopped. He slipped off his captain's armband and gave it to Abbas. "Your friend is captain of Hall United," Claude said. "You should be captain of Grandview."

"Are you sure?" Abbas asked. Being captain was a big honour.

"Yes, I have a feeling. But only if you win the coin toss!"

Abbas hurried over the ref standing with Victor. They were both waiting for him.

"Congratulations," the ref said. "You both deserve to be here. Hall, clearly you are home team. Heads or tails?"

"Heads," Victor said as the ref flipped the coin.

"Heads it is. Hall United will kick off."

"I thought I told you to win the coin toss!" said Claude to Abbas.

"Let's win the game instead," Abbas replied as the team came in for a cheer.

"Let's go Eagles! Play hard! Play safe! Play fair!"

With a sharp blast of the whistle the final game

began. Sam sent the ball quickly back to Hassan, one of Hall United's midfielders.

Grandview formed up their defence. Like the Eagles, Hall United played a 4-4-2 formation. Each team had two strikers, four midfielders, and a wall of four defenders protecting the goalkeeper.

"Watch out!" shouted Claude.

Hall United's Dylan was making a run down the sideline toward the Eagle's goal. Mo moved to cover.

Their plan ruined for now, Hassan passed the ball back to Riad. Riad was a Syrian boy and the tallest fullback on Hall United. He slowly dribbled up the field, looking, waiting for one of his midfielders or strikers to get open.

Dylan rushed toward him. Riad was not expecting the sudden attack and quickly passed the ball toward Tarek. His kick was not quite on target and Abdul intercepted it. Grandview had control of the ball.

Both teams were fighting their nerves. Abdul sent the ball to Claude who quickly passed it along to Abbas, halfway between the centre line and the Hall United crease. Excited or nervous or both, Abbas took a shot from almost thirty metres out.

The ball sailed through the air, bouncing on the turf five metres away from Victor. Victor caught it easily on the first bounce.

"You're going to have to do better than that, Abbas," he called. He rolled the ball quickly on the ground to Owen, Hall's fullback.

"Plenty of time," Abbas replied. "You'll be seeing me again soon."

But Abbas couldn't take another shot on Victor for the rest of the first half. Most of the play was in the middle of the field. The defenders on both teams played very well, like a tall wall protecting their goalkeepers.

Dylan would come the closest to scoring for the Eagles. Michael booted the ball high and hard into the air. Sunny, a Hall United midfielder, misjudged where it would land. He watched helplessly as the ball bounced over his head. Dylan took advantage of the mistake and shot downfield toward the goal.

A defender came forward, but before he could challenge for the ball, Dylan blasted it toward Victor.

It was a beautiful shot, one of the best Dylan had ever made. The ball flew toward the net, curving to the left corner. Almost any other time on any other goalie it would have been a goal.

But Victor was no ordinary goalkeeper. He saw the path of the curving ball and adjusted quickly. He leaped into the air, catching it in his sure hands.

Dylan groaned as he watched Victor make the save. The half was nearly over and his shot had been the closest either team had come to scoring.

Just two minutes later, Tarek picked up the ball from a pass from Riad and quickly sent it over to Sunny. He didn't misjudge the ball this time. He sent it up to Sam, Hall United's other striker, with a beautiful header.

It was Grandview's turn to make a mistake, and they would pay for it. Sam charged toward Michael, the Eagles goalie. Alvin and Steven raced toward him, certain that he would shoot.

Sam didn't shoot. Instead he made a quick deke, faked out both Eagles defenders and chipped the ball to Hall United's Dylan. That Dylan sent the ball hard and fast across the turf toward the right corner. Michael read the play correctly but the ball was too fast for him to reach. Abbas watched in horror as it rolled over the goal line.

Hall United: 1, Grandview: 0.

Thirty seconds later the referee blew his whistle. The first half was over.

21
Top Flight

The Eagles felt deflated as they walked off the pitch. The game had been so close. Having Hall United score like that with almost no time left in the half made them feel terrible. Even Claude, always so upbeat, looked upset. He knew that as team captain it was his job to rally them.

Then Abbas remembered that for this game at least, he was the captain. His friends had helped him get to the tournament. He could help them play their best.

"Shake it off, Eagles," he said. "They got lucky. We have thirty minutes left. We can do it. We didn't come all this way to get down on ourselves now. I may not be Claude but I have a feeling we are going to get an equalizer very quickly!"

"Abbas is right," said Coach T. "One goal is nothing, even against these guys. Have some water, take a breath and refocus."

"Thanks, Abbas," Claude said, his grin returning. "You're right. We have plenty of time left." He turned to the rest of the team. "You heard our mighty captain!" he announced. "Let's get back out there and do this!"

Five minutes into the second half, Abbas's feeling came true. Junior took a beautiful lob from Claude on the centre line and quickly flicked it up to Dylan. Dylan took the ball in his feet and sprinted toward Victor.

Riad and Owen were caught flat-footed. There was a gap between them. It wasn't more than three metres, but Dylan saw it and slipped through.

Victor squared up to face the shot. Dylan faked right. Victor bent his knees and moved ever so slightly in the same direction. It was enough. Quickly Dylan pulled the ball to the left, blasting it waist high. Victor tried to adjust, quickly diving to the left.

The shot was hard. It hit Victor's fingertips. But his fingertips didn't stop it. The ball flew into the mesh at the back of the net. Victor lay on the turf, watching in disbelief.

Hall United: 1, Grandview: 1.

"What did I tell you?" Abbas said as the Eagles lined up at centre field.

The rest of the second half played out like a chess match. Neither team took chances on offence or defence. They were so evenly matched that both teams knew one simple mistake could quickly lead to a goal. As the minutes dragged by there was little doubt the next goal would be a golden goal, regulation time or not.

Hall United came closest to scoring with just a few minutes to go.

"Pass!" shouted their striker, Sam. He'd found a hole between Jun and Claude and streaked through it. Tarek saw him and sent a beautiful ball toward him.

Abbas could hardly breathe as he watched Sam, ball on his boots, head toward Michael. Hall United had scored on a play just like this at the end of the first half. To have them do it again would be heartbreaking.

Sam shot, a strong blast that went high, clearing the top bar of the net by a good three metres. Sam hung his head in his hands, shocked that he missed such a chance.

"You'll get it next time!" cheered Victor from the other end of the field. But there was no next time, at least not in regulation.

Soon after Michael kicked the ball downfield to resume play, the referee blew his whistle.

"Looks like it's golden goal in extra time to win again," said Coach T as the players came off the pitch. "Any feelings about the outcome this time, Claude? Last time we needed a golden goal, you said Abbas would score it against Regent Heights. And you were right."

"Nothing," panted Claude. He'd been running up and down the field non-stop for an hour. "No feelings.

All I know is that whoever scores a goal in the next five minutes will win the game."

"And that will be us," said Dylan. "One more goal and Top Flight is ours!"

But Dylan's prediction didn't come true. The five minutes of extra time did not settle the game. Both teams were tired and so nervous they could hardly breathe. They played safe, avoiding risky passes, not doing anything that could cost them the championship.

Tweet! The ref blew his whistle to end extra time.

Varsity Stadium was buzzing with excitement. Both teams had played each other to a draw. Love it or hate it, they were moving on to penalty kicks. Nothing in soccer was more exciting.

"Captains!" called the referee. It was time for one last coin toss, to see who would try to score first.

"Somehow I knew it would come to this," said Victor, shaking Abbas's hand. "I'm glad you're here. I'm glad you got on that plane."

"Me too," Abbas said. "You beat me in my hometown. Now it's my turn to repay the favour."

"Grandview, you make the call this time," said the ref, taking out his loonie.

"Heads," Abbas called. He watched as the golden coin flipped through the air and landed on the turf.

"Heads it is. What do you want to do, Grandview?"

"We'll kick first," Abbas said. It was what Coach T had told him to say if he won the toss.

Coach T set the kicking order. Dylan would go first, followed by Claude and then Abbas. If they won the shootout, odds were good that it would be on Abbas's turn.

"All right then," the referee said. "Good luck to both of you. And may the best team win."

Abbas realized he wasn't nervous at all. And all his fears were gone. No matter what happened, he and his team were strong. He and Victor were true friends. It was the best feeling in the world.

"Don't worry," said Abbas and Victor at the same time. "We will!"

Acknowledgements

I would like to thank Kat Mototsune for her incredible editing skills. I would also like to thank James Lorimer for supporting refugee learners and readers. Additionally I owe a deep debt of gratitude to the ELL teaching staff, settlement workers and community coordinators of Edmonds Community School and Byrne Creek Community School. As always, thanks to my wife Sharon for her love and support.